Rogue

The Honorable Rogues®, Book One

COLLETTE CAMERON

Blue Rose Romance®
Portland, Oregon

Sweet-to-Spicy Timeless Romance®

A KISS FOR A ROGUE
The Honorable Rogues®, Book One
Copyright © 2014 Collette Cameron
Cover Design by: Darlene Albert

This book is a work of fiction. Names, characters, places, and incidents are the product of the author's imagination or are used fictitiously. Any resemblance to actual events, locales, or persons, living or dead, is coincidental.

All rights reserved under International and Pan-American Copyright Conventions. By downloading or purchasing a print copy of this book, you have been granted the non-exclusive, non-transferable right to access and read the text of this book. No part of this text may be reproduced, transmitted, downloaded, decompiled, reverse engineered, or stored in or introduced into any information storage and retrieval system, in any form or by any means, whether electronic or mechanical, now known or hereinafter invented without the express written permission of copyright owner.

Attn: Permissions Coordinator
Blue Rose Romance®
8420 N Ivanhoe # 83054
Portland, Oregon 97203

eBook ISBN: 9781954307360
Paperback ISBN: 9781954307377
www.collettecameron.com

"Then why did you leave?"
"Why did you let me go?"

"Beautiful chemistry...You'll cheer for these star-crossed lovers."
Christi Gladwell USA Today Bestselling Author

Other Collette Cameron Books

The Honorable Rogues®
A Kiss for a Rogue
A Bride for a Rogue
A Rogue's Scandalous Wish
To Capture a Rogue's Heart
The Rogue and the Wallflower
A Rose for a Rogue

Check out Collette's Other Series
Castle Brides
Highland Heather Romancing a Scot
Daughters of Desire (Scandalous Ladies)
The Blue Rose Regency Romances:
The Culpepper Misses
Seductive Scoundrels
Heart of a Scot

Collections
Lords in Love
The Honorable Rogues® Books 1-3
The Honorable Rogues® Books 4-6
Seductive Scoundrels Series Books 1-3
Seductive Scoundrels Series Books 4-6
The Blue Rose Regency Romances-
The Culpepper Misses Series 1-2

Dedication

For the sweetest lady I know.

Friend, encourager, prayer warrior, and woman of God.

Acknowledgements

A Kiss for a Rogue is my first attempt at a novella, and my first trip down the self-publishing road. I wasn't even sure I could write a novella, but as always, my wonderful Regency critique partners said to go for it. And to the most amazing reader group ever, **Collette's Chéris**, who daily prove what generous, giving, and supportive people readers are.

Bless each and every one of you!

xoxo

Collette

A lady must never forget her
manners nor lose her composure.
~*A Lady's Guide to Proper Comportment*

1

London, England
Late May, 1818

"This is a monumental mistake."

God's toenails. What were you thinking, Olivia Kingsley, agreeing to Auntie Muriel's addlepated scheme?

Why had she ever agreed to this farce?

Fingering the heavy ruby pendant hanging at the hollow of her neck, Olivia peeked out the window as the conveyance rounded the corner onto Berkeley Square. Good God. Carriage upon carriage, like great shiny beetles, lined the street beside an ostentatious manor. Her heart skipped a long beat, and she ducked out of sight.

Braving another glance from the window's corner, her stomach pitched worse than a ship amid a hurricane. The full moon's milky light, along with the mansion's rows of glowing diamond-shaped panes, illuminated the street. Dignified guests in their evening finery swarmed before the grand entrance and on the granite stairs as they waited their turn to enter Viscount and Viscountess Wimpleton's home.

The manor had acquired a new coat of paint since she had seen it last. She didn't care for the pale lead shade, preferring the previous color, a pleasant, welcoming bronze green. Why anyone living in Town would choose to wrap their home in such a chilly color was beyond her. With its enshrouding fog and perpetually overcast skies, London boasted every shade of gray already.

Three years in the tropics, surrounded by vibrant flowers, pristine powdery beaches, a turquoise sea, and balmy temperatures had rather spoiled her against London's grime and stench. How long before she grew accustomed to the dank again? The gloom? The smell?

Never.

Shivering, Olivia pulled her silk wrap snugger. Though late May, she'd been nigh on to freezing since the ship docked last week.

A few curious guests turned to peer in their carriage's direction. A lady swathed in gold silk and dripping diamonds, spoke into her companion's ear and pointed at the gleaming carriage. Did she suspect someone other than Aunt Muriel sat behind the distinctive Daventry crest?

Trepidation dried Olivia's mouth and tightened her chest. Would many of the *ton* remember her?

Stupid question, that. Of course she would be remembered.

Much like ivy—its vines clinging tenaciously to a tree—or a barnacle cemented to a rock, one couldn't easily be pried from the upper ten thousand's memory. But, more on point, would anyone recall her fascination with Allen Wimpleton?

Inevitably.

Coldness didn't cause the new shudder rippling

from her shoulder to her waist.

Yes. Attending the ball was a featherbrained solicitation for disaster. No good could come of it. Flattening against the sky-blue and gold-trimmed velvet squab in the corner of her aunt's coach, Olivia vehemently shook her head.

"I cannot do it. I thought I could, but I positively cannot."

A curl came loose, plopping onto her forehead.

Bother.

The dratted, rebellious nuisance that passed for her hair escaped its confines more often than not. She shoved the annoying tendril beneath a pin, having no doubt the tress would work its way free again before evening's end. Patting the circlet of rubies adorning her hair, she assured herself the band remained secure. The treasure had belonged to Aunt Muriel's mother, a Prussian princess, and no harm must come to it.

Olivia's pulse beat an irregular staccato as she searched for a plausible excuse for refusing to attend the ball after all. She wouldn't lie outright, which ruled out her initial impulse to claim a *megrim*.

"I ... we—" She wiggled her white-gloved fingers at her brother, lounging on the opposite seat. "Were not invited."

Contented as their fat cat, Socrates, after lapping a saucer of fresh cream, Bradford settled his laughing gaze on her. "Yes, we mustn't do anything untoward."

Terribly vulgar, that. Arriving at a *haut ton* function, no invitation in hand. She and Bradford mightn't make it past the vigilant majordomo, and then what were they to do? Scuttle away like unwanted pests? Mortifying and prime tinder for the gossips.

"Whatever will people *think*?" Bradford thrived on upending Society. If permitted, he would dance naked as a robin just to see the reactions. He cocked a cinder-black brow, his gray-blue eyes holding a challenge.

Toad.

Olivia yearned to tell him to stop giving her that loftier look. Instead, she bit her tongue to keep from sticking it out at him like she had as a child. Irrationality warred with reason, until her common sense finally prevailed. "I wouldn't want to impose, is all I meant."

"Nonsense, darling. It's perfectly acceptable for

you and Bradford to accompany me." The seat creaked as Aunt Muriel, the Duchess of Daventry, bent forward to scrutinize the crowd. She patted Olivia's knee. "Lady Wimpleton is one of my dearest friends. Why, we had our come-out together, and I'm positive had she known that you and Bradford had recently returned to England, she would have extended an invitation herself."

Olivia pursed her lips.

Not if she knew the volatile way her son and I parted company, she wouldn't have.

A powerful peeress, few risked offending Aunt Muriel, and she knew it well. She could haul a haberdasher or a milkmaid to the ball and everyone would paste artificial smiles on their faces and bid the duo a pleasant welcome. Reversely, if someone earned her scorn, they had best pack up and leave London permanently before doors began slamming in their faces. Her influence rivaled that of the Almack's patronesses.

Bradford shifted, presenting Olivia with his striking profile as he, too, took in the hubbub before the manor. "You will never be at peace—never be able to move on—unless you do this."

That morsel of knowledge hadn't escaped her, which was why she had agreed to the scheme to begin with. Nevertheless, that didn't make seeing Allen Wimpleton again any less nerve-wracking.

"You must go in, Livy," Bradford urged, his countenance now entirely brotherly concern.

She stopped plucking at her mantle and frowned. "Please don't call me that, Brady."

Once, a lifetime ago, Allen had affectionately called her Livy—until she had refused to succumb to his begging and run away to Scotland. Regret momentarily altered her heart rhythm.

Bradford hunched one of his broad shoulders and scratched his eyebrow. "What harm can come of it? We'll only stay as long as you like, and I promise, I shall remain by your side the entire time."

Their aunt's unladylike snort echoed throughout the carriage.

"And the moon only shines in the summer." Her voice dry as desert sand, and skepticism peaking her eyebrows high on her forehead, Aunt Muriel fussed with her gloves. "Nephew, I have never known you to forsake an opportunity to become, er ..."

She slid Olivia a guarded glance. "Shall we say, become better acquainted with the ladies? This Season, there are several tempting beauties and a particularly large assortment of amiable young widows eager for a *distraction*."

Did Aunt Muriel truly believe Olivia don't know about Bradford's reputation with females? She was neither blind nor ignorant.

He turned and flashed their aunt one of his dazzling smiles, his deeply tanned face making it all the more brighter. "All pale in comparison to you two lovelies, no doubt."

Olivia made an impolite noise and, shaking her head, aimed her eyes heavenward in disbelief.

Doing it much too brown. Again.

Bradford was too charming by far—one reason the fairer sex were drawn to him like ants to molasses. She'd been just as doe-eyed and vulnerable when it came to Allen.

"Tish tosh, young scamp. Your compliments are

wasted on me." Still, Aunt Muriel slanted her head, a pleased smile hovered on her lightly-painted mouth and pleating the corners of her eyes. "Besides, if you attach yourself to your sister, she won't have an opportunity to find herself alone with young Wimpleton."

Olivia managed to keep her jaw from unhinging as she gaped at her aunt. She snapped her slack mouth shut with an audible click. "Shouldn't you be cautioning me *not* to be alone with a gentleman?"

Aunt Muriel chuckled and patted Olivia's knee again. "That rather defeats the purpose in coming tonight then, doesn't it, dear?" Giving a naughty wink, she nudged Olivia. "I do hope Wimpleton kisses you. He's such a handsome young man. Quite the Corinthian too."

A hearty guffaw escaped Bradford, and he slapped his knee. "Aunt Muriel, I refuse to marry until I find a female as colorful as you. Life would never be dull."

"I should say not. Daventry and I had quite the adventurous life. It's in my blood, you know, and yours too, I suspect. Papa rode his stallion right into a church and actually snatched Mama onto his lap moments before she was forced to marry an abusive lecher. The scandal, they say, was utterly delicious." The duchess sniffed, a put-upon expression on her lined face. "Dull indeed. *Hmph*. Never. Why, I may have to be vexed with you the entire evening for even hinting such a preposterous thing."

"Grandpapa abducted Grandmamma? In church, no less?" Bradford dissolved into another round of hearty laughter, something he did often as evidenced by the lines near his eyes.

Unable to utter a single sensible rebuttal, Olivia swung her gaze between them. Her aunt and brother beamed, rather like two naughty imps, not at all abashed at having been caught with their mouth's full of stolen sweetmeats from the kitchen.

She wrinkled her nose and gave a dismissive flick of her wrist. "Bah. You two are completely hopeless where decorum is concerned."

"Don't mistake decorum for stodginess or pomposity, my dear." Her aunt gave a sage nod. "Neither permits a mite of fun and both make one a cantankerous boor."

Bradford snickered again, his hair, slightly too long for London, brushing his collar. "By God, if only there were more women like you."

Olivia itched to box his ears. Did he take nothing seriously?

No. Not since Philomena had died.

Olivia edged near the window once more and worried the flesh of her lower lip. Carriages continued to line up, two or three abreast. Had the entire *beau monde* turned out for the grand affair?

Botheration. Why must the Wimpletons be so well-received?

She caught sight of her tense face reflected in the glass, and hastily turned away.

"And, Aunt Muriel, you're absolutely positive that Allen—that is, Mr. Wimpleton—remains unattached?"

Fiddling with her shawl's silk fringes, Olivia attempted a calming breath. No force on heaven or earth could compel her to enter the manor if Allen were betrothed or married to another. Her fragile heart, though finally mended after three years of painful healing, could bear no more anguish or regret.

If he were pledged to another, she would simply take the carriage back to Aunt Muriel's, pack her belongings, and make for Bromham Hall, Bradford's newly inherited country estate. Olivia would make a fine spinster; perhaps even take on the task of housekeeper in order to be of some use to her brother. She would never set foot in Town again.

She dashed her aunt an impatient, sidelong peek. Why didn't Aunt Muriel answer the question?

Head to the side and eyes brimming with compassion, Aunt Muriel regarded her.

"You're certain he's not courting anyone?" Olivia pressed for the truth. "There's no one he has paid marked attention to? You must tell me, mustn't fear for my sensibilities or that I'll make a scene."

She didn't make scenes.

The *A Lady's Guide to Proper Comportment* was most emphatic in that regard.

Only the most vulgar and lowly bred indulge in histrionics or emotional displays.

Aunt Muriel shook her turbaned head firmly. The bold ostrich feather topping the hair covering jolted violently, and her diamond and emerald cushion-shaped earrings swung with the force of her movement. She adjusted her gaudily-colored shawl.

"No. No one. Not from the lack of enthusiastic mamas, and an audacious papa or two, shoving their simpering daughters beneath his nose, I can tell you. Wimpleton's considered a brilliant catch, quite dashing, and a top-sawyer, to boot." She winked wickedly again. "Why, if I were only a score of years younger ..."

"Yes? What *would* you do, Aunt Muriel?" Rubbing his jaw, Bradford grinned.

Olivia flung him a flinty-eyed glare. "Hush. Do not encourage her."

Worse than children, the two of them.

Lips pursed, Aunt Muriel ceased fussing with her skewed pendant and tapped her fingers upon her plump thigh. "I would wager a year's worth of my favorite pastries that fast Rossington chit has set her cap for him, though. Has her feline claws dug in deep, too, I fear."

Displaying envy or jealousy
reflects poor breeding; therefore, a
lady must exemplify graciousness at all times.
~*A Lady's Guide to Proper Compartment*

2

D^{uty.}

An heir apparent must marry.

Allen snagged a flute of champagne from a passing servant.

Bloody well wish it were a bottle of Sethwick's whisky.

Part Scots, Viscount Sethwick boasted some of the finest whisky Allen had ever sampled. The champagne bubbles tickling his nose, he took a sip of the too sweet, sparkling wine and, over the crystal brim, canvassed the ballroom.

Which one of the ladies should he toss his handkerchief to and march down the aisle with?

A posturing debutante, beautiful and superficial?

A cynical widow, worldly-wise and free with her favors?

A shy chit past her prime but possessing a fat dowry?

Or perhaps a bluestocking or a suffragist who preferred reading books and carrying on discourses about women's oppression rather than marry? At least with the latter he could have intelligent conversation about something other than the weather and a bonnet's latest accoutrements.

He really didn't give a damn—didn't care a wit who he became leg-shackled to or who the next Viscountess Wimpleton would be. The only woman he'd loved had left England three years ago, and he hadn't heard from Olivia since. His gut contracted and shriveled up.

So much for forgiveness and love's enduring qualities.

Livy's gone and not coming back. You drove her away and now must pick another bride.

Familiar regret-laced pain jabbed Allen's ribs, and he clamped his jaw. He had been an immature arse, and the consequence would haunt him the remainder of his miserable, privileged life. Heaving a hefty breath, he forced his white-knuckled grip to relax before he snapped the flute's stem.

Mother, no doubt, was pleased as Punch at the crush attending his parents' annual ball. If too many more guests made an appearance, the house might burst. Devilishly hot, the ballroom teemed with overly-perfumed, sweaty—and the occasional unwashed—bodies.

God, what he wouldn't give for a more robust spirit than this tepid champagne. The weak beverage did little to bolster his patience or goodwill. At this rate, he would be a bitter curmudgeon by thirty. A drunkard, too. Given the brandy he'd imbibed prior to coming down stairs, he was half-way to bosky already.

After finishing the contents in a single gulp, he lifted the empty glass in acknowledgement of his mother's arched brow as she pointedly dipped her regally coiffed head toward Penelope Rossington.

He might not give a parson's prayer who he wed, but his parents did. She must be above reproach, and if Mother thought Miss Rossington suitable ...

Responsibility.

Allen had an heir to beget.

Miss Rossington was pretty enough, exquisite some might say, and generously curved too. Her physical attributes made her quite beddable. She was also dumb as a mushroom and shallow as a snowflake. He'd had more intelligent conversations with barmaids.

He cocked his head as she gave him a coquettish smile before murmuring something to her constant companions, the dowdy and turnip-shaped Dundercroft sisters. They giggled and turned an unbecoming, mottled shade of puce.

A practiced flirt, Miss Rossington had recently become possessive of him and exhibited an unflattering jealous streak. Still, she would do as well as any other, he supposed, since those behaviors seemed universally present in the *ton's* marriageable females.

Allen released a soft snort. He never used to be so

judgmental and jaded.

Exchanging his empty flute for another full one—only his third this evening—he caught his mother's troubled expression. She pulled on Father's arm before lifting onto her toes and fervently whispering in his ear.

Father speared him a contemplative glance, and Allen raised his glass once more.

Cheers. Here's to a bloody miserable future.

His parents couldn't fathom his cynicism since theirs had been a love match.

Frowning, Father murmured something and patted Mother's hand resting atop his forearm.

Casting Allen a glance, equally parts contemplative and maternal, she nodded before smiling a welcome to Bretheridge and Faulkenhurst, two of Allen's university chums.

Steering his attention overhead, Allen contemplated the gold plasterwork ceiling and newly painted panels adorned with dancing nymphs and other mythical creatures. Mother had begun massive redecorating shortly after Olivia Kingsley had left. He'd always suspected she had done so to help erase Olivia's memory.

Bloody impossible, that.

Fully aware Olivia had ripped Allen's heart from his chest and hurled it into the irretrievable depths of the deepest ocean, his parents worried for him. They also fretted for the viscountcy's future if he didn't shake off his doldrums and get on with choosing a wife.

Propriety.

He'd always been the model of decorum.

Tedious, dull, snore-worthy respectability.

Except for a single time when he had rashly shoved aside good sense, Allen had always heeded his parents' and society's expectations. Never again would he indulge such an impulse. His position required he attend these damnable functions, dance with the ladies, and ensure the Wimpleton name remained untarnished. Bothersome as attending the assemblies was, pretending to enjoy himself proved Herculean, though, he had become quite adept at the subterfuge.

Copious amounts of spirits helped substantially,

but drowning self-recriminations in alcohol fell short of noble behavior, or so his Father had admonished on numerous occasions, most recently, this afternoon.

Finally acquiescing to his parents' gentle, yet persistent prodding, Allen had set his attention to acquiring, what would someday be, the next viscountess. Another blasted obligation. Those not borne into the aristocracy didn't know how fortunate they were, especially only sons.

However, once he had made his choice, he needn't feel obligated to attend as many social functions, and when he did appear, he could spend the evening in the card room, or better yet, escape to the study with a few coves and indulge in a dram or two.

Maybe he and his bride would retire to the country, at least until the title became his—not that he wished his father into an early grave or was overly eager to assume the viscountcy. Since seeing the magnificent horseflesh bred at Sethwick's castle, Craiglocky, Allen had considered entering into a cattle breeding venture of his own. Surely that would keep his mind occupied with something other than melancholy musings.

His wife would want for nothing except his affections. Those weren't his to give. A certain tall, fiery-haired goddess possessing sapphire eyes had laid claim to them, and his love would forever be entangled in her silky chestnut hair. But he would be a kind and faithful husband. He quite looked forward to dangling his children upon his knee, truth to tell.

An image of a chubby-cheeked imp with sea-blue eyes and wild cinnamon curls sprang to mind. On second thought, he did have one stipulation for his future wife. She could not have red hair.

Taking a sip of champagne, he rested a shoulder against a pillar.

Miss Rossington glided his way, a coy smile on her rouged lips, and if he wasn't mistaken, a bold invitation in her slanted eyes. Her dampened gown left little to his imagination, and though she wore virginal colors, he would bet the coat on his back, she'd long ago surrendered her maidenhead.

He quirked his mouth. Perhaps, she wouldn't do after all. Though he must wed, he didn't relish cuckoldom.

Barely suppressing an unladylike curse, Olivia gave her aunt the gimlet eye. Did she say a year's worth of pastries? Hound's teeth, then it was a given. Aunt Muriel took her pastries very seriously, as evidenced by her ample figure.

Olivia scowled then immediately smoothed her face into placid lines.

Ladies do not scowl, frown, or grimace.

Or so Mama had always insisted, quoting *A Lady's Guide to Proper Comportment* as regularly as the sun rose and set from the time Olivia was old enough to hold her own spoon.

She hadn't quite decided how to go about competing for Allen's affections, if any chance remained that he still cared for her. Perhaps she should ask Aunt Muriel for advice.

On second thought, that might prove disastrous. Her aunt had already suggested a clandestine kiss. No telling what scandalous, wholly inappropriate notion Aunt Muriel would recommend. Why, Olivia might find herself on the edge of ruin in a blink if she followed her aunt's advice.

Tonight, she would find out precisely where she stood with Allen, whether she dared still hope or should concede defeat and accept her heartbreak. Just what kind of woman was she up against, though? "No doubt this Rossington miss is excessively lovely."

If only Aunt Muriel would say she's homely as a toad with buggy eyes and rough, warty skin. Oh, and Miss Rossington was missing several teeth and had a perpetual case of offensive breath.

"Hmph. If you consider a heavy hand with cosmetics, dampened gowns, and bodices that nearly expose entire bosoms lovely, I suppose she is." Aunt Muriel resumed her preening.

Bradford's mouth crept into a devilish smile. "I quite like dampened gowns—"

"Brady!" Olivia kicked his shin. Sharp pain radiated from her slippered toe to her knee. *Bloody he—*

Proper ladies do not curse, Olivia Antoinette Cle-

opatra Kingsley! Mama's strident voice admonished in Olivia's mind.

"—and exposed bosoms." Brady risked finishing, nestled in the carriage's corner with his arms crossed and a mouth-splitting, unrepentant grin upon his face.

He enjoyed quizzing her, the incorrigible jackanape.

"Of course you do." Aunt Muriel lifted her graying eyebrows. The twitch of her lips and the humor lacing her voice belied any true censure. "My poor sister would perform one-handed somersaults in her grave if she knew what a rogue you have become, always up to your ears in devilry. Don't know where you got that bend. Your father was as stiff and exciting as a cold poker, and your mother never did anything remotely untoward, always quoting that annoying comportment rubbish."

Another rogue dominated Olivia's thoughts.

What if Allen dismisses or cuts me?

The possibility was quite real.

She had no reason to believe he might yet hold a *tendre* for her, but she most know for certain, no matter how devastating or humiliating. She feared her rehearsed speech would flit away the moment she opened her mouth, leaving her empty-headed and tongue-tied, and although she had attempted to prepare for a harsh rebuff, practicing imaginary responses couldn't truly ready her for his or the *ton's* rejection and scorn.

As the carriage lurched to a rumbling stop, she sent a silent prayer heavenward. No stars, dim from the new gas streetlamps before the mansion and the coal-laden clouds blanketing London shot across the sky for her to wish upon. It had been on a night very much like this that she'd been a young fool and crushed her and Allen's dreams of a future together. However, in her defense, she had only known him for a blissful fortnight before he proposed.

Already completely taken with Allen, she'd become teary-eyed during a waltz and shared her dismay. In a matter of days, her father intended to move the family to the Caribbean for a year. Father hadn't given them any notice or time to prepare, just announced, in his impulsive, eccentric way, that they were off to Barbados to oversee a sugar plantation. She had been full of girlish hopes and dreams, and Father's plans severed them at the root.

What maggot in his brain had possessed him to buy a plantation? He had known nothing of farming or harvesting, preferring fossils and rocks to humans and their usual activities. Even Olivia's Season could be ascribed to a deathbed vow Father had made to Mama; one he had repeatedly attempted to renege on until Bradford had intervened on Olivia's behalf.

She had long suspected Father never intended for her to marry, but to remain at his side as his companion, housekeeper, and nurse until his days ended.

Closing her eyes, she pictured that romantic dance three years ago.

Allen had held her closer than propriety dictated, but not so much as to be ruinous. After whisking her onto the veranda, he'd captured her hand, and they had sped to a garden alcove. Whether he'd planned to ask her, or had been caught up in the moment and spontaneously decided to, she would never know, but he had hurled convention to the wind, dropped to one knee, and after promising to love her for eternity, asked her to share the rest of his life.

She had loved him almost from the first moment she'd seen him standing across the ballroom, sable head thrown back and laughing unrestrained. Her chest welling with emotion, she had tossed aside her mother's constant harping on proper comportment as carelessly as used tea leaves, and said yes, even though Papa wouldn't have approved.

Olivia hadn't cared.

Especially when Allen had smiled, his countenance full of joy, and then had sealed their troth with a scorching kiss. Her nipples pebbled and a jolt of arousal heated her blood as recollection of their potent embrace produced a familiar response. A quick survey of her wrap assured her that her body's reaction remained a secret, and Aunt Muriel and Bradford hadn't a hint of her sensual musings.

That had been the happiest moment of her life, and the cherished memory elicited a tiny, secretive smile.

Then, Allen had revealed his intention to elope to Gretna Green.

That night.

Taken aback at his impetuous suggestion, uncertainty had niggled, its sharp barbs pricking and stirring her misgivings. Mother had died a year ago, and Father suffered from ill-humors. It might have been too much for his frail health if Olivia had eloped. She had thought to have a few weeks, months perhaps, before wedding Allen. Besides, a fortnight wasn't enough time to truly fall in love—not a deep, abiding, eternal love, was it?

More than enough time when your soul finds its other half.

She breathed out a silent, forlorn sigh. Her silly doubts had fueled her fear of making a hasty, impulsive decision. And so, regretfully, she'd said no to hieing off to Scotland, and instead, asked him to wait a year for her to return to England.

"We could write back and forth, truly get to know one another and plan for our future together. A year isn't so very long." She tried to persuade Allen to wait. "Many couples are betrothed for a lengthy period."

Setting her from his embrace, his answer had been

an emphatic, "Like hell I shall. I love you and want to marry you now, not in a year, dammit. That's a bloody eternity."

"But, I cannot elope tonight." She touched his arm, trying to reclaim the happiness of a moment before but, shoulders and face stiff, he had turned away from her. "It's too sudden, Allen, and I'm worried what the shock would do to Papa."

Head bowed, his forearm braced against the arbor entrance, and his other hand resting on his narrow hip, Allen had spoken, his voice so raspy and quiet, she had strained to hear him.

"If you really loved me, you wouldn't want to wait to marry. You would be as eager as I am." Dropping his hands to his sides, he faced her, his voice acquiring a steely edge. "It seems I have misjudged your affection for me. Go to the Caribbean. I won't try to dissuade you again."

He had left her standing, crushed and weeping, in the arbor. Wounded at his callousness, after regaining her composure, she had made her way to the veranda where she'd encountered Allen's sister, Ivonne. Claiming to feel unwell, Olivia had asked her to find Father and Bradford and tell them to meet her at the entrance. Betrayal fueling her anger, she hadn't even bid her hosts farewell.

It wasn't until the ship was well out to sea did she realize, she hadn't ever told Allen she loved him. Not a day had passed since sailing that she hadn't lamented not eloping. Wisdom had arrived too late, and she had destroyed her greatest opportunity for love and happiness.

Maybe my only opportunity.

No doubt the torturous road to Hades was paved with a myriad of regrets, for life without him would surely be—*had been*—hell.

A white-gloved footman in hunter green livery opened the door. He set a low stool before the carriage and smiled. "Good evening, Your Grace."

"Good evening, Royce. My nephew will see us alighted." Aunt Muriel waved her hand at another carriage where a large woman teetered within the doorway. "Go help over there before Lady Tipples topples onto the pavers and cracks them." A grin threatened.

"Tipples topples. Didn't plan that. Funny though."

"At once, Your Grace." After bowing, Royce dashed to the other conveyance. He and another footman managed to wrangle the squawking woman, swathed in layers of orange ruffles and bows, onto the pavement.

"Wouldn't mind her absence tonight, truth to tell." Jutting her chin toward the commotion, Aunt Muriel slipped her reticule around her wrist. "She always wants to bore me with the latest clap trap or her current revolting ailment. I heard more about gout and constipation last week than a body ever needs to know."

Chuckling, Bradford descended first then turned to hand Aunt Muriel down.

Hands clasped so tightly, her fingers tingled, Olivia remained rooted to her seat, her attention fixed on the entrance.

Allen is in there.

Bradford stuck his head inside the carriage. All signs of his former joviality gone, he regarded her for a long moment, kindness crinkling the corners of his eyes. He chucked her beneath her chin.

"Come along, Kitten. Put on a brave smile, and let's go meet the dragon. I dare say the past three years have been awful for you, always wondering if Wimpleton still cares. Who knows, mayhap tonight is providential. In any event, you'll have an answer, and you can get on with your life."

Bradford had suffered the loss of his first love, and his facade of a carefree, womanizing rake, hid a deeply injured man. If anyone understood her plight, it was he.

"I suppose that's true." Although her existence would be only a shadow of what life might have been with Allen.

Such a pity hindsight, rather than foresight, birthed wisdom.

Bradford extended his hand. "Let's be about it then."

Sighing, and resigned to whatever providence flung her way, Olivia placed her palm in his. "All right."

"That's my brave girl." He gave her fingers a gentle, encouraging squeeze.

Not brave. Wholly terrified. "So help me, Brady, you step more than two feet away from me, and I shall—"

"Never fear, Kitten. I shall forsake my romantic pursuits and act the part of a diligent protector for the entire evening. I but lack my sword to slay your fears."

Despite her rioting nerves, Olivia grinned. "How gallant of you, dear brother, and a monumental sacrifice, at that."

"Indeed. A selfless martyr." Sarcasm puckered Aunt Muriel's face as if she had sucked a lemon. "For certain he's deemed for sainthood now."

"Anything for you, Liv. You know that." He tucked Olivia's hand into the crook of one elbow while offering the other to their aunt before guiding the women up the wide steps. A few guests smiled and nodded in recognition as the trio entered the manor.

Olivia forced her stiff lips upward and reluctantly passed her wrap to the waiting footman. Had he detected her shaking hands? The scarlet silk mantle provided much more than protection from the spring chill; it shrouded her in security. Her stomach fluttered and leaped about worse than frogs on hot pavement, threatening to make her ill.

She ran her hands across her middle to smooth the champagne-colored gauze overlay of her new crimson ball gown Aunt Muriel had insisted on purchasing. The ruby jewelry she wore was her aunt's as well.

Though Bradford, now the newly titled Viscount Kingsley, had inherited a sizable fortune, Olivia had balked at acquiring a new wardrobe. "My gowns are perfectly fine. I'll simply wear a shawl or mantle until I become accustomed to England's clime once more."

Besides, if she didn't reconcile with Allen, she was leaving London, and a wardrobe bursting with the latest frilly fashions was a senseless waste of money as well as useless for country life.

"Chin up and smile, Livy. You look about to cast up your crumpets." Bradford clasped her elbow, as if lending her his strength.

Casting up her accounts was the least of her worries. Swallowing her panic, she offered him a grateful smile as they stood before the butler.

"Her Grace, the Duchess of Daventry, Lord Kingsley, and Miss Kingsley." The majordomo announced them in the same droning monotone he had the previous guests.

Behind Olivia, someone gasped.

Perfect.

A low murmur of hushed voices circled the room in less time than it took to curtsy as the three of them advanced into the ballroom. Perhaps Bradford's rise in status caused the undue interest. After all, he had been third in line to the viscountcy, and if their curmudgeon of an uncle and two cousins hadn't drowned in a boating accident, Brady would have been spared a title he disdained.

Combing the room from beneath her lashes, her stomach lurched.

Every eye was trained upon them. Her. At least it seemed that way from the brief glimpse she had braved.

This is a mistake.

Head lowered and her attention riveted on the polished marble floor, she prayed for strength. Where was the pluck Papa had praised her for, or the feistiness

Bradford often teased her about? Or the spirit Allen had so admired?

She could do this. She must if she were ever to discover the truth. Otherwise, not knowing would badger and pester her, preventing her from ever finding the peace she craved.

Had Allen forgotten her? Did he love another now? That Miss Rossington?

There was only one way to find out.

Olivia forced her eyes upward. Inhaling, she squared her shoulders, commanded her lips to tilt pleasantly, and lifted her head.

Her gaze collided squarely with Allen's flabbergasted one.

A lady of gentle-breeding should
never appear too eager to engage the
attentions or affections of a gentleman.
~*A Lady's Guide to Proper Comportment*

3

What the hell is she doing here?

Allen damned near dumped his champagne down Miss Rossington's ample bosom upon hearing Olivia's name announced. Unprepared to see the woman he had once loved more than he had thought humanly possible standing in his home again, her presence had blindsided him.

Utterly lovely, staring at him, her eyes startled and huge, Olivia's beauty clobbered him with the same force as a horse's kick to the gut. Those huge, Scottish beasts Sethwick's sister raised with hooves the size of carriage wheels.

Vises clamped his heart and squeezed his lungs as whooshing echoed in his ears, wave after wave, in accompaniment to his frantic heartbeat. Perspiration broke out across his upper lip and beaded his forehead. He didn't need a looking glass to know he had gone white as new-fallen snow.

For one very real moment, he couldn't suck in an ounce of air and feared he would swoon. Wouldn't that give the quartet of chinwags standing by the potted ficus something to bandy about? Especially Lady Clutterbuck, the worst gossipmonger in Town.

Say, did you see Wimpleton? Keeled over like an ape-drunk sot.

That he had taken to imbibing freely for some time now would lend credence to the tattle.

Tiny blackish specks frolicked before his eyes, and the roaring in his ears became deafening.

Breathe, man.

Jaw rigid, he marshaled his composure and dragged in a painful, inadequate breath, then another. The blood thrumming in his ears lessoned a degree.

One more ragged breath and his vision cleared a

mite.

Olivia's presence sent him hurtling back to the evening she had announced her father's intention to move her family to Barbados— *in two bloody days*.

Desperate not to lose her, and willing to endure censure and scandal, Allen had thrown his pride aside and implored her to flee to Scotland with him that very night. His one instance of selfish impulsiveness. Look how well that had turned out.

Now, she hovered, hesitant and anxious, at the ballroom's entrance, and a tidal wave of devastation and hurt crashed down upon him, drowning him in remorse. It took every ounce of self–control to regard her impersonally.

One hand pressed to her throat, Olivia looked positively wan—terrified even.

Hell's teeth. She better have a damned good reason for showing up on her aunt's coattails.

When had the Kingsleys returned to England? Why hadn't anyone told him? Warned him?

Likely because he had been absent from London the previous week, overseeing the delivery of some prime horseflesh to Wyndleyford House, their country estate. He'd only returned to London this morning.

The duchess, stately as any queen, perused the ballroom. Her regard lit on Allen for an extended moment, and she dipped her head, her mouth arcing before her scrutiny gravitated onward.

No blatant snub from her grace. Well, at least that was something.

Allen fought dual impulses. One, to turn on his heel, giving Olivia the cut direct, and the other, to charge across the room, sweep her into his embrace, and beg her forgiveness in front of everyone.

Only she had the ability to make him act recklessly, and the last time he'd done so hadn't gone all that well. No. Much wiser to keep his distance, pretend she hadn't once been his reason for living, and focus on his pursuit of an acceptable bride.

Miss Rossington clawed at his arm, her citrine eyes sparking with jealousy, and her ruby-tinted lips tightly pursed. She looked about to fly into one of her starts.

"Who is she? I don't recall seeing that creature before." She squinted, her tightly furrowed brows forming a vee between her eyes. "Egads, she's a longshanks, isn't she? Probably starves herself to stay that slender. And would you look at her hair? Colored, to be sure, just like a lady of the night."

Her almond-shaped eyes tapering to slits, she tittered with feline satisfaction. Haughtiness turned her striking features into an over-indulged, petulant child's.

What did she know of ladies of the night?

He took a half-step back and took her measure, as if finally seeing her for the first time.

Deuce take it.

Allen cupped the back of his neck where a pair of cannon balls seemed to have taken up residence. Was he addled? He had half-heartedly contemplated courting this hellcat. Large bosoms and a beautiful face didn't compensate for a narrow mind and spiteful shallowness.

"Men prefer a woman with curves, or so I've been told." She rubbed her breasts against his arm, fairly purring. This was no innocent miss, but a woman skilled in using her physical charms. Very experienced, or he missed his mark. "She's a bit long in the tooth, isn't she?"

Allen clamped his jaw, his nostrils flaring, as she hurled yet another insult at a woman she had never met. It said much about her character. ... Or lack, thereof.

His too, that he had slid to such depths, that he would have ever considered tainting the Wimpleton name, his family's heritage and exemplary standing, with a trollop like Penelope Rossington just so he could put the distasteful task of marriage behind him.

That had been before Olivia's unexpected return.

Now the notion of making a match with Miss Rossington was as welcome as gargling hot coals. Allen contemplated his half-full champagne flute. More fine bubbles floated to the top and popped. Truthfully, a union with anyone except Olivia held as much appeal.

How could he still want her?

His treacherous eyes searched her out again, a brilliant scarlet bloom in a bouquet of pale pinks, creamy ivories, and chaste whites.

How could he not?

"Do you know who the gentleman with her is?" Miss Rossington practically licked her lips as she ogled Kingsley. "He seems far superior in breeding. Perhaps she's a poor relation—"

"He's her brother. Her name is Olivia Kingsley, and she's ..." He paused and looked at Miss Rossington.

She glared at Olivia, jealousy distorting her face.

My God, such a bratling.

"How old are you?" Odd, he'd never wondered at her age before.

Miss Rossington shifted her focus to him and elevated her chin. Her green eyes flashed with confidence, even as a seductress's smile bent her overly-rouged mouth. "Eighteen. Almost nineteen."

The same age as Livy when we met.

He tipped his lips at the edges. The termagant clutching his arm was about to receive a proper set down. "She only boasts three years on you, and I assure you, that *is* her natural hair color."

From the corner of his eye, he covertly scrutinized the crowd. Most of the guests had made a pretense of resuming their activity prior to the announcement of the Kingsleys' and duchess's arrival.

Olivia had drawn the consideration of nearly everyone present. Beauty such as hers commanded recognition, though she would be the first to decry the attention. Modest, she'd never seen the exquisiteness in her looking glass others did when gazing upon her. Maneuvering her way along the perimeter of the crowded ballroom, her brother and aunt, like alert sentinels, guarded her.

Rather, the Duchess of Daventry, much like a schooner, the wind filling its canvases, sailed forth, parting the seas before them. With furled brows and piercing gazes, she and Kingsley cowed the more brazen or insolent guests who dared to stare at Olivia outright.

Though her face held a placid expression, Olivia's stiff posture and the firm set of her shapely mouth revealed she was well-aware of the murmurs behind fans and hands directed her way. Her vibrant coppery hair and ruby jewelry shone beneath the glowing chandeliers, but Allen detected vulnerability in her sooty-lashed eyes.

His heart pinched painfully at her discomfort. Why he should care a whit about her feelings was beyond him, and that he yearned to comfort and protect her rankled him no end. A man should be able to control his deuced, capricious emotions, yet his disloyal heart—what was left of the mangled organ after she had shattered it to hell and back—ached for her.

Nodding at something Kingsley said, the bronze highlights in Olivia's cinnamon hair glinted like dark honey.

Allen had always adored her glorious hair. "The color of her hair is splendid, is it not?"

Miss Rossington released an irritated huff, her talon-like fingers tightening on his forearm. Clearly, she did not agree. "And how would you know about her dull hair? Rusty nails shine brighter. Assuredly that shade is not God-given." Accusation rang in her petulant voice, and his estimation of her dove lower. "Women of her ilk are quite skilled at artifice."

You ought to know.

Taking Miss Rossington's measure, he gave himself a violent mental shake. God spare him title-hungry viragos with the morals of a bitch in heat. She had become much too possessive of late, and her disparaging Olivia was beyond the mark.

Yes. It was far past time to put Penelope Rossington in her place and disabuse her of any notion she was viscountess-worthy, once and for all. If ever a woman was beneath the privilege, it as she.

Feeling far freer than he had in a long while, Allen took a deep breath and notching his chin, he caught site of his mother poised, statue-still, her focus riveted on Olivia.

Her eyes round as tea saucers, Mother's gaze traveled from Olivia, lingered on Miss Rossington for a fraction then drifted back to Olivia once more. She unfurled her fan, and Allen swore he saw her grin—a face-splitting show of white teeth—before she began frenetically waving the fan and bustled toward Father, shoving guests aside in her haste.

"Well, don't you intend to answer me, Allen?" Miss Rossington's voice rose shrilly with all the charm and appeal of someone chewing glass. "How do you know her?"

Allen handed his flute to a passing footman. "It isn't any of your concern, but I shall indulge you anyway."

And quite enjoy your reaction.

He peeled her claws from his arm, finger by finger, and once free, smoothed his wrinkled coat sleeve.

"Olivia Kingsley is the woman I almost married."

Other than her gloved hands,
at no time should any part of a lady's
form touch a gentleman's while dancing.
~*A Lady's Guide to Proper Comportment*

4

*A*llen.

Olivia's heart cried silently across the distance as she ravenously scoured every inch of him from his burnished hair to his gleaming shoes, before returning to his adored face. Their gazes locked, and time hung suspended for an intense, agonizing moment.

"Olivia, stop gawking. People will think you're fast or desperate." Speaking under her breath, Aunt Muriel nudged her. "Come along. Let's find a seat, shall we?"

Olivia dragged her gaze from Allen, and Bradford took her by the elbow. Skirting the guests, they wove their way through the crush toward the black Trafalgar chairs bordering one side of the ballroom.

Allen was exactly as she remembered—ruggedly handsome and wholly irresistible.

With an utterly exquisite young woman on his arm.

Using her brother as a shield, Olivia covertly eyed Allen, drinking him in with her gaze.

Attired in black, except for a scarlet and silver waistcoat, he exuded maleness. High cheekbones framed a nose too strong to be considered aristocratic, but his lips were perfectly sculpted.

She had tasted those delicious lips once. So long ago. She touched her mouth with her gloved fingertips in remembrance.

"Olivia!" Aunt Muriel hissed from the side of her mouth while smiling and inclining her head at acquaintances as she sailed forth, towing Olivia in her wake. She squeezed Olivia's elbow when she didn't respond immediately. "Put your hand down. Compose yourself at once. I'll not have you disparaged for acting the ninny."

Olivia pretended to scratch her upper lip—indelicate, but a far cry better than pressing her fingers to her mouth—then dropped her hand, her attention still locked on Allen. "But, Aunt Muriel, you said you wanted Allen to kiss me. Surely that's scandal-worthy."

"True, but an indiscretion in a secluded nook is a far cry from making a spectacle in full view of the *beau monde*. A lady can do exactly what a strumpet does, the difference being, she doesn't carry on in the street." Exchanging nods with a dour-faced peeress, Aunt Muriel steered Olivia forward and muttered an almost inaudible, "Lady Clutterbuck. A pedantic fussock, and the worst tattlemonger in all London."

Adopting a smile, Olivia spared the dame a glance, nearly recoiling at the disapproval lining the woman's close-set eyes and, pouting fish lips. No ally there.

A group of arrogant, young bucks swaggered toward a cluster of giggling debutants, and Olivia seized the opportunity to sneak another look at Allen. His thick, sable hair swept across a high brow, accented his heavy-lashed malachite eyes. He had the most arresting eyes she had ever seen on a man. An errant lock curled over his tanned forehead, giving him a rakish air. Even across the room, his unusual green eyes glinted with something powerful.

Umbrage? Anger? Outrage?

Her step faltered, and she swallowed, not at all positive that what glistened in the depths of his gaze was hospitable. For certain, the black look his lovely companion glared at Olivia radiated hostility.

Miss Rossington?

"Buck up, Kitten. The *ton* is watching, their pointed teeth bared and ready to attack anyone showing the least weakness." Bradford whispered the warning in her ear as he led her to a trio of empty seats along what had once been a peach and ivory silk-draped wall, now a sunny primrose yellow.

Lady Wimpleton had recently redecorated and refurbished the inside of the mansion too.

Everything was much the same, yet different as well. Rather like Olivia and Allen. She stole another glance at him. His dark visage offered her no quarter, and her legs gone weak, she sank thankfully onto a chair.

Yes, indeed, this was the worst possible idea. Rather like setting sail upon the ocean in a leaky skiff.

During a tempest.

Without provisions.

Naked and blind.

Perhaps she would seek out the ladies' retiring room and spend the next hour or two cloistered there.

"Ah, I see Lady Pinterfield." Aunt Muriel indicated a woman wearing copious layers of puce and black, almost as garishly attired as she. "I need to speak with her. Her chef concocts the most delicious ratafia cakes. I simply must acquire the recipe, though she's been impossibly difficult to persuade to part with it. I haven't given up yet, mind you. I shall invite her to tea to sample her very own recipe. She cannot refuse me then." Pulling a face, Aunt Muriel sighed. "I suppose I can be persuaded to endure her company for an hour in exchange for those delicacies."

With a fluttering wave, she all but bolted toward the unsuspecting woman.

Olivia gave a closed-lip smile as Aunt Muriel

swooped in on her startled prey. Heaven help Lady Pinterfield if she still wasn't eager to share the recipe.

True to his word, Bradford, after snaring a flute of champagne from a cheerful footman, took a position beside an enormous, cage-shaped potted ficus to Olivia's left.

Several twittering damsels openly ogled him, lust in their not-so-innocent eyes.

He curved his lips into a knowing smile and gave them a roguish wink.

A chorus of thrilled giggles and blushes followed, and then a quiet buzz hummed as they bent their heads near and a flurry of whispering commenced with an occasional bold peek from below fluttering lashes.

Others—older, more experienced ladies—spoke behind their fans to one another or, with a seductive curving of their painted mouths, brazenly stared.

His grin widened as he leaned, ankles crossed, against the wall and perused the assembled female guests from beneath his hooded eyes. He quite enjoyed the reactions he garnered.

Incorrigible scapegrace.

At six and twenty, he ought to stop behaving recklessly, but to do so meant he had put Philomena's memory aside. That wasn't something Olivia was certain he would ever be able to do. He had been just shy of twenty when Philomena had died, but he'd truly loved her. Still did, for that matter.

Olivia and Bradford made quite the pair, both doomed to suffer for their lost loves, although a large portion of Olivia's misery could be attributed to her own making.

A young woman pointed at her and snickered.

Tendrils of heat snaked from Olivia's neck to her cheeks. Edging her chin up a degree, she whipped her fan open. Waving it briskly, she surreptitiously studied Allen and attempted to ignore the not-altogether-kind feminine tittering further along the neat row of chairs. Let them prattle. She didn't count any of them as friends. Groups had gathered in nearly every open space, and from one, several gentlemen scrutinized her, likely trying to decide whether to ask her to dance.

Please don't.

To discourage their attentions, she angled her back

toward them. Not that she didn't enjoy dancing—she rather adored the pastime, especially the waltz. It had been three years since she'd attended any event with dancing as part of the entertainment, but tonight, she only cared to partner with one man.

Deliberately turning even farther away from their appraisal, she caught her breath.

No. It cannot be.

A woman bearing a striking resemblance to Philomena disappeared through the French windows.

Impossible. Utter piddle.

Olivia had become so flustered upon seeing Allen, she now imagined things. See what the man did to her?

Allen stood across the ballroom, his stance rigid and his countenance an unreadable mask. He didn't acknowledge Olivia's presence with as much as a blink or a nod.

That stung. More than she cared to admit. She had attempted to brace herself for this response but underestimated how painful the actual rejection would be.

She flapped her fan faster, her grip on the slender handle tight enough to snap the fragile wood. Well, what had she expected? That he had forgiven her and would charge across the ballroom, take her in his arms, and profess his undying love in full view of all?

Yes. Though unrealistic, far-fetched, and idealistic, that is what she'd hoped for.

It would have been wonderful—more than wonderful—an answer to three years' worth of desperate prayers. Instead, it appeared he intended to disregard her. To give her the cut. He had never been cruel before, which proved how much she'd wounded him.

Deeply. Irrevocably. Permanently

A crest of disappointment engulfed her, and a sob rose from her chest to her throat as stinging tears welled in her eyes.

I will not cry. I. Will. Not!

Not here. Not now.

She wouldn't give the gossips the satisfaction. Later, in her bedchamber, when no prying or gloating gazes could witness her heartache and mortification, she would indulge in a good cry. One final time. Then, she would dry her eyes, square her shoulders, and march, head held high, into her lonely future.

Like waves to the shore, Allen drew her perusal once more. He held a champagne glass in one hand, his other arm commandeered by that stunning, petite blonde.

Olivia quirked her lips into a cynical smile. At five feet ten inches, and with a head of unruly auburn hair, she was neither petite nor blonde. Nor nearly as curvaceous as the creature clinging to Allen, gazing at him with adoration, her full breasts crushed against his arm.

Ridiculously huge breasts, truth to tell.

Did she stuff her gown? How did her small frame support those monstrosities? With her nipples poking forth so, it was a wonder she didn't topple forward onto her face and crack the parquet flooring with them.

The blonde shifted away from Allen slightly, bringing Olivia's less than charitable musings to a screeching halt.

She blinked in disbelief.

Were those ...?

No. They couldn't be.

Olivia's jaw loosened, but she managed to prevent it from smacking against her chest.

She squinted at the girl's bosom.

Yes. They were.

Dual earth-toned circular shadows were clearly visible through the gown's light fabric.

Good God. Wasn't she wearing a chemise?

Parading about naked beneath one's gown, displaying one's ware like a Friday night harlot was beyond the pale.

The woman peered up at Allen, her countenance enraptured, and blister it, from where Olivia sat, he appeared as entranced as the young lady. Or maybe it was the blatant display of womanly attributes he found spellbinding.

Her bountiful bosoms certainly held numerous other gentlemen's rapt attention.

Dropping her gaze to her beaded, crimson slippers, jealousy nipped Olivia, sharp and deep. Scorching tears pricked behind her eyelids again, and hiding behind her fan's protection, she shut them.

Too late. I'm too confounded late.

She drew in a shuddery breath, willing her eyes to stop pooling with moisture.

Well, that was that. Bradford could find their aunt while Olivia waited in the carriage. At least she knew Allen's feelings now, but the knowledge brought her no respite.

"Miss Kingsley, may I request the pleasure of a dance?"

Startled, Olivia eyes popped open, and she clutched her throat, her fan tumbling to the floor. Allen had approached, rapid and soundless. And oh, so very welcome.

Where had the female barnacle gotten to? The way she had clung to Allen, Olivia doubted the chit had been pried loose voluntarily and was likely vexed. Offering a poised, albeit timorous smile, she peered past his black-clad muscled form as he straightened from his bow.

Ah, there she was, attached to another attractive gentleman, so scandalously close a starving flea couldn't have squeezed between them if the insect held its breath. Her cat-eyes sparked with irritation as she took Olivia's measure before turning her back in an intentional snub.

Had she some claim to Allen? An informal promise? A secret betrothal?

Olivia's stomach and hope withered.

"Has another requested the next dance?" Allen's melodious baritone drew her ponderings back to him.

Olivia opened her mouth, but her mind went blank—empty as a beggar's purse, just as she had feared.

Then dear Bradford was there, picking up her brisé fan and saving her from her gaucheness. "No. No one has requested a dance with my sister as yet. You are the first."

Bradford!

He avoided looking at Olivia as he stood upright. "Of course she would be delighted to accept your offer."

She chastised him hotly with her gaze.

Just you wait, Brady, you traitorous toad.

After returning the accessory to her, he extended his hand to Allen. "Good to see you, Wimpleton."

Allen smiled and clasped her brother's palm. He seemed genuinely pleased to see Bradford. They had been good friends before the Kingsley's departure.

"Likewise, Kingsley. Are you finding London's temperature a mite cool after your time in the tropics? No doubt you're eager to return to the milder climate." Green fire burned in the gaze he slid Olivia as he uttered the last slightly clipped words.

His stinging innuendo met its mark, and she flinched inwardly but refused to let him see he had affected her. Rather amazed at her ability to appear composed, she met his cool regard.

"We're not returning, Mr. Wimpleton. After Papa died last year, Bradford sold the plantation."

Allen's forehead creased in momentary surprise, and then he swiftly schooled his expression. "I heard of your loss. Please accept my condolences."

"Thank you." She inclined her head and another bothersome curl flopped free.

Dratted hair.

Allen's lip twitched. He'd forever been tucking stray tendrils behind her ears or helping her re-pin errant strands. More than once, he had expressed the wish to see her hair down.

Bradford grinned, his attention directed across the room. "Olivia, since Wimpleton is partnering you for this dance, I've a mind to reacquaint myself with his sister and ask her to introduce me to that delectable creature standing beside her."

Olivia followed his regard.

A ravishing brunette wearing a stunning lavender-pink gown burst out laughing at something Ivonne said. The raven-haired beauty really ought to be warned, so she could flee before Bradford ensnared her. Poor dear. Once under his spell, women usually stuck fast, like ants in molasses, for a good while.

Until he broke their heart.

He didn't do it intentionally, but when they became too clinging, their sights set on marriage, he gently severed his association. Only, they didn't always willingly go their own way, and then he was forced to brusqueness.

"Behave yourself, Brady."

He chuckled wickedly and wagged his eyebrows. "Always, Kitten."

With a devilish wink and half-bow, he took his

leave and sauntered away.

So much for gallant promises.

His expression somber, Allen extended his hand, palm upward. "The waltz is about to begin. Shall we?"

Olivia stared at his outstretched hand.

Did she dare? Wasn't this why she had come?

Now was as good a time as any to test the waters. Sink or swim. Unable to take a decent breath, she did feel she was drowning, especially when she gazed into his eyes. Intense emotion simmered there, and her pulse quickened in response. She inhaled, an inadequate, puny puff of air. Mayhap her new French stays were to blame for her breathlessness.

Fustian rubbish.

Allen was to blame.

The musicians' first strains echoed loudly in the oddly quiet room. Perhaps he commanded all her senses, and everything else had faded into the background.

"Miss Kingsley? The waltz, if you please?" Allen's soft prompt steadied her nerves.

"Yes, of course." Summoning a tremulous smile, Olivia placed her equally shaky fingers in his hand and allowed him to assist her to her feet. His unique scent—crisp, spicy, yet woodsy—smacked her with the force of a cudgel.

She inhaled deeply, savoring his essence as he tucked her hand into the bend of his elbow and led her onto the sanded floor.

A path opened before them. Like the parting of the Red Sea, several other couples moved aside, allowing them to pass, a few speculating openly as she and Allen walked by.

She had anticipated the *ton's* long memory but found it discomfiting, nevertheless.

Prickles along her spine warned her that dozens of guests watched their progress, some not at all pleased with the turn of events. A quick glance over her shoulder confirmed Miss Rossington's pinched face and fuming gaze.

Precisely what was Allen's relationship with the woman?

Please God, don't let them be betrothed.

He bowed, and Olivia curtsied, somehow managing to keep from teetering over from nerves. The floor soon filled with other couples, many of whom craned their necks and rudely gawked in her and Allen's direction. She felt rather like a curiosity at Bullock's Museum; a peculiarity to be stared at and discussed.

Why couldn't they mind their own business? She conceded this public reunion might not have been the wisest course after all, but the bread had been put to rise and there was no unleavening it now.

Allen took her in his arms, his stance too near to be considered wholly respectable. Nonetheless, she melted into his arms, reveling in their familiarity and comfort, much like returning home after a lengthy journey, which ironically, she had just done.

Shoulders stiff and coolly silent, he began circling them about the room.

He's angry.

Olivia peeked up at him through her eyelashes.

He looked straight ahead, his jaw clenched and a scowl pulling his eyebrows together.

No. He's livid.

While she couldn't get enough of him, he barely tolerated touching her. Why had he asked her to dance when he obviously struggled as much with her proximity as she did his, though for entirely different reasons?

For appearances? To prove she meant nothing to him?

She should never have come to the ball.

Such utter foolishness to think something might be salvaged of their love. She would endure this dance with some semblance of dignity, and afterward, she would make short work of finding Bradford and Aunt Muriel. They would bid their hosts a hasty farewell, and Olivia would leave her dreams of happiness and reconciliation behind forever.

Expertly guiding her between two couples, Allen's shoulder muscles stiffened even more when she clutched him during a complicated turn. Relaxing her grip, she tried to ease away, to put a bit of distance between them. He either ignored her effort or was so lost in his thoughts and discomfort, he didn't respond to her subtle attempts.

Like strangers forced to spend time together, silence loomed, awkward and heavy. She and Allen had never had trouble talking before. In fact, their ease at conversing is one of the first things that attracted her to him. Now a cavernous chasm, eroded by years of separation, misunderstanding, and hurt divided them.

Nibbling her lower lip, she strove for something sensible to say, but all coherent thought had vanished the instant he touched her. His hand upon her back branded her with possessive heat, and each time his thighs brushed her gown, her legs responded by going weak in the knees.

Ridiculous things.

Ridiculous her.

For pity's sake. Allen was just a man, not a god with divine powers capable of mesmerizing the fairer sex. True, he was the first man to hold her in his arms in years, and the only one she ever wanted to from now until eternity flashed to an end, but she reacted like a wanton.

She concentrated on counting in time to the waltz's lilting strains—*one, two, three, one, two, three*—in an attempt to keep her mind occupied, but her cluttered thoughts hurtled around, bouncing off each other, dissonant and jarring, like church bells clanging on Sunday morning.

How could she have been so naïve as to think they might put the last three years behind them? While she had remained trapped in the Caribbean, caring for her dying father, Allen had gone on with his life. A tiny sigh escaped Olivia at the injustice, but then fate never claimed to be a mistress of fairness.

The lulling music wound its way around her taut nerves until she became lost in the music and gradually began enjoying the dance. She truly did adore dancing. With him.

She closed her eyes, remembering another waltz, where she and Allen had danced indecently close. Cheeks heated by the recollection, she opened her eyes and searched Allen's dear face. Though tall herself, she had to look up to meet his eyes.

He still stared at some point beyond her, tension ticking in his jaw.

His slightly spicy scent wafted past her nostrils again, flooding her senses. She stifled the impulse to bury her nose in his neck and kiss his throat, but she couldn't help drawing in another deep breath and inhaling his essence, not only into her lungs, but into her spirit.

These last treasured moments, dancing with him, were all she would ever have, and she was determined to savor each one fully.

Did he hold the minutest trace of warm regard for her still, or had his disappointment and anger irrevocably hardened his heart? Did he remember that fateful evening—their dance and kiss too?

His focus lowered, lingering on her lips for a brief moment. His nostrils flared, and his molded mouth tightened.

Yes. He remembered.

His expression closed and unreadable, except for the amber shards sparking in his eyes, he met her gaze. "Why are you here? Did you think to take up where we left off?"

Infinite care and consideration should be
given when a lady chooses her words and
even more so when she elects to speak them.
~*A Lady's Guide to Proper Comportment*

5

Allen cursed inwardly for asking Olivia the confounded question. He'd sworn to himself he would ask her to dance, uncover her scheme, and send her on her way. Completely unaffected, he would then go about his life and she about hers.

What a colossal, stinking pile of horse manure.

"You humiliated me, Olivia, practically leaving me at the altar."

Holy hell, do stubble it.

She gasped and stumbled, and he tightened his embrace, steadying her.

Her azure gaze, huge and alarmed, flitted about

the room, probably seeking a means of escape. The tip of her pink tongue darted out and touched the pillow of her lower lip. "That's not true. We hadn't told anyone of our plans to marry. You had just proposed. No one knew."

He ought to give her that, but his anger wouldn't allow any concession.

The moment he'd seen her standing in the entry, he had sworn he wouldn't acknowledge, let alone speak to her. Olivia was none of his concern. She held no interest any longer. He didn't want anything more to do with her. When she had chosen her father over him and left to go gallivanting off in the tropics, he'd slammed that door closed and drove the bolt home.

Ballocks, you unmitigated liar. You love her every bit as much as you did the night you rejected her.

His tongue, fueled by offended pride, paid his conscience no heed. "There were wagers on White's books, betting we would wed by summer's end. The entire *bon ton* recognized me as a besotted fool."

Maybe not the entire *ton*, but a sizable number had.

Olivia's beautiful eyes widened in wounded shock, and her lower lip quivered the tiniest bit before she dropped her thick-lashed gaze to stare at his shoulder.

The pulse in her throat beat erratically, and she trembled. "I beg your pardon. This dance was a mistake. Please return me to my aunt or brother."

"Like hell I will." He grated the words out beneath his breath, his voice a harsh rasp.

She stiffened and looked about, half panicked.

Dragging in a juddery lungful, he hauled his attention back to his surroundings. At the end of the opulent, overheated ballroom, his parents stood beside the Duchess of Daventry, concern etched upon their countenances.

They feared he would make a scene.

He feared he would make a bloody scene.

Allen had never been this out of control before. Olivia's presence had damned near knocked him head over arse, and he still hadn't completely recovered his composure.

Drawing in another fortifying gulp of air, he

forced a smile to his taut lips and nodded at the gawkers stretching their necks to see what transpired between Olivia and him.

Bloody ballroom full of giraffes and ostriches.

Allen would've loved to tell the lot to bugger off.

Instead, he elevated a brow and leveled them a civil, yet quelling look.

Dancing nearby, Miss Rossington jerked her attention away with such abruptness she mashed her partner's foot. Tripping, the man muttered an oath and bumped into another couple. They too, faltered before regaining their balance.

An amusing vision of the dancers tumbling over like stacked cards, one after the other, and ending in a writhing pile of arms and legs upon the floor flashed before Allen. The corner of his lips skewed upward. It would give the guests something to blather about other than him and Olivia.

"Mr. Wimpleton, I demand you release me at once." Her face constrained, Olivia attempted to pull away. She gave his shoulder a small shove. "Let go."

She had tried that earlier, too, but he held her fast,

craving her nearness. Desperately, dammit.

"Cease." He bent his neck, his mouth near her small ear. Another inch and he could trace the delicate shell with his tongue. How would she react if he did? He drew in an extended breath. God, she smelled divine. Warm, and flowery with the faintest hint of citrus. The creamy column of her neck beckoned, as did the silky spot just below her ear, and the velvety hollow at the juncture of her throat.

He swallowed, lest he give into the urge to trail his lips from one, to the other, to the other. "We shall finish this waltz, and you shall smile and pretend to enjoy the dance. I'll not intentionally give the gossipmongers a single morsel to toss about at my expense ever again."

Casting the dancers a sidelong glance, she stopped trying to escape. Her lips ribbon thin, she shook her head. A russet tendril sprang loose, toppling onto her ear. "Too late for that, I'm afraid. My being here has stirred that unpleasant pot into a bubbling froth. I never should have come. It was foolish of me."

"Why did you?"

"I ..." Her shoulders slumped, and she tucked her chin to her chest. "I wanted to see you."

He had to strain to hear her whispered words.

Her head sank lower. "Just one more time."

As simple as that. No pretense. No expectations or demands.

Was it possible Olivia had missed him as much as he had missed her? Despite his reservations, his treacherous heart rejoiced. Words were beyond him at the moment, and swallowing, he canvassed the room.

Mother poked Father with her fan and sent the duchess a sly, knowing smile at something her grace said.

The Duchess of Daventry looked much too pleased.

By thunder. Did she just wink at him? Had she orchestrated this?

Given her reputation for being unconventional and high-handed, he shouldn't be the least surprised. Befuddled, he wasn't sure whether to thank or curse her.

Allen edged Olivia even closer, until the crown of her head almost touched his chin. Despite insisting he release her a moment ago, she didn't resist.

Her light perfume tormented him, shooting a blast of sensation to his loins and sending his lust soaring. Hound's teeth, as if his manhood bulging in his breeches wouldn't cause more whispers and titters. And trying to dance with a stiffened rod bumping against one's leg presented an uncomfortable challenge.

Women didn't realize their good fortune in wearing skirts, for their arousal didn't tent their trousers—bloody apparent for the world to see.

Sixty seconds in his arms and Olivia had him at sixes and sevens.

And hard as marble.

Only she had this power over him. Even after an extended absence from her, he responded like a wet-behind-the-ears pup with his first woman.

Well done, old man. Your self-control is pitiable.

He dismissed his musing. All that mattered was this moment and holding her in his arms. Caressing the curve of her rib, Allen guided her through another difficult turn, made more so by the blatant eavesdroppers pressing near.

A slight smile edging her mouth, she unerringly followed his lead.

They had always been superb dance partners, and he hadn't a doubt she would have been unequaled as a bedmate. He'd been eager to introduce her to passion's promises once she became his wife.

His already-stirred member jerked, yanking his attention back to the present. He scrutinized Olivia through half-closed eyes.

She had grown even more beautiful.

Her gorgeous red hair, untamed and wild, like her, was streaked with gold, no doubt from exposure to the tropical sun. A jeweled ruby band peaked between artfully arranged curls—curls every bit as silky as they appeared.

Her eyes, the clearest ocean blue he'd ever seen, stayed riveted on his neckcloth. Her unique gown—cherry-red with an overlay somewhere between ivory and light gold—enhanced her glowing skin, giving her an almost ethereal appearance. Few red-heads dared wear crimson tones, but she managed to look exquisite in the becoming gown. A slight pout marred her pretty lips, slightly damp and pinkened from being nibbled, and vexation creased her usually smooth brow.

She possessed a woman's figure now. Her breasts were fuller, the creamy mounds surging above the neckline of her gown hinting at the treasures hidden beneath the fabric. Treasures he longed to sample. No, was desperate to taste and touch.

Fiend seize it, he had thought himself over her, and truth to tell, feared ever again experiencing the pain her betrayal caused him. He'd drowned himself in drink and staggered about half-foxed for a month after her departure. If he was honest, he taken to drinking too much since, as well.

The waltz's steps brought them near the French window at one end of the ballroom. The terrace doors stood wide open, summoning him. Before his conscience had a chance to raise an objection or dared to spout good sense, Allen whirled Olivia out the opening, just like he had that fateful night.

She stopped dancing at once and pulled from his embrace, glowering at him.

Not the same as three years ago.

"This is most improper." She attempted to step past him and reenter the house, but he blocked her path. Her color high, she glared at him. "I must return inside immediately or my reputation will be compromised."

"Not until I've spoken my piece." Allen grasped her elbow, preventing her escape. Intent on seeking a private bower, he glanced swiftly around before releasing her elbow only to clasp her hand.

"Allen, let me go." Eyes narrowed, she wriggled her fingers. "You cannot go about dragging ladies here and there willy-nilly at your pleasure."

His pleasure? Not by a long shot.

"Don't kick up a fuss. I simply want to talk without a score of ears listening to my every word." He steered her down the narrow flagstone steps and onto the lawn. Lanterns dotted the landscape, bathing the flowers and shrubberies in a warm glow, and where the lanterns couldn't penetrate the darkness, the moon's silvery beams provided a subtle half-light to all but the remotest recesses.

A woman's giggle echoed from somewhere within the garden. Seemed he wasn't the only one intent on bit of air and privacy. Her laughter sounded again, likely from the arbor further along the curving path that split the lawn as neatly as parted hair. A few stolen kisses might be had there away from the sharp eyes of the dowagers and watchful mamas.

"What are you doing?" Olivia tugged at her hand clamped within his. "Are you trying to ruin me? You just said you didn't want any more gossip. You don't think this," she gave another yank and bobbed her head toward the veranda, "won't signal the rumormongers that something's afoot?"

That halted Allen in his tracks. Standing in the center of the manicured garden, he scanned the area. They were fully visible to the few guests taking the air on the terrace, but far enough away that no one could easily overhear their conversation. Her reputation would remain intact, and he could say what he had burned to say since she stepped into the ballroom.

"I'm sorry I came tonight. It's evident my presence has upset you. That was never my intent." Olivia released a jerky breath, misery etched upon her lovely face. "Please let me return to the house, and I shall leave at once and not bother you with my presence again."

"Not yet." He shook his head and straightened his waistcoat before slanting her a wry glance. "I must confess, I am grateful I didn't wait the year you asked for, Livy." He leaned closer, holding up three fingers. "Since it has taken three for you to reappear on the London scene."

Gasping, she flinched as if struck. Her gaze faltered, but not before raw pain darkened her eyes, and she took a reflexive step back.

He released her hand. Hell, he was an unmitigated, chuckleheaded ass.

"I didn't think you wanted me to return." She lifted her chin a notch, her incredible blue eyes lancing him with accusation. "I remember your words from that night quite clearly, Allen."

God, he remembered, too, every grating, cold syllable spewing from his lips. Guilt and shame kicked him in the ribs, pulverizing his pride.

She stared at a point beyond his shoulder, her eyes swimming with tears. She blinked several times, and swallowed audibly, obviously attempting to control her emotions. Her voice hoarse, she repeated his hateful words.

"'Don't expect me to wait for you, Olivia. If you choose your father over me, we're finished.'"

A lady of refined breeding will,
at all times, avoid raising her voice or
engaging in public displays of histrionics.
~*A Lady's Guide to Proper Comportment*

6

"Olivia, I ..."

Allen reached for her once more. He mustn't cause her more anguish, must make amends for his cruelty. In that moment, he hated himself, hated what love had turned him into.

Olivia lurched away, hiding her hands behind her back.

Did she fear him? A knife, jagged and rusty, twisted in his bowels.

Poised to flee, distrust lurked in her gaze—her gorgeous eyes that had once sparkled with adoration.

He had done this to her, yet he had suffered equally. "Not one letter in three years. I assumed you had stopped loving me."

"You made no attempt to contact me either, Allen. You're the one who said we were finished. Surely, you knew the Duchess of Daventry had our address. For all I knew, you had married by now." The sorrow in her voice ripped at his gut.

"There's never been anyone else, Livy."

Never would be, either. He cast a swift glance over his shoulder. No one seemed to pay them any heed, unless ... He squinted. Unless that was Mother hiding amongst the draperies beside the French Windows. No. The figure was larger than Mother. Her Grace? He suppressed a chuckle. The woman knew no bounds.

Perhaps he could convince Olivia to join him in the library or Father's study to finish this conversation. Who knew who might be loitering in the shrubberies, eavesdropping on their every word? This discussion was too private to have bandied about by a loose-tongued tattlemonger.

"What about Miss Rossington?" Lips pursed,

Olivia darted a telling glance toward the manor. "She seemed quite attached to you. I didn't imagine the darkling glowers she showered upon me."

He shook his head again, noting Olivia's high color. Was she jealous? The notion gave him a jot of hope. A disinterested woman didn't harbor envy.

"Her father and mine attended Oxford together. She's a guest of my parents, that's all, no more important than the bevy of other woman they have invited tonight."

Close enough to the truth, for Allen had never entertained any serious intentions regarding the chit. A drunkard's ale lasted longer than his brief foray into insanity when he had fleetingly considered courting her. She had proved an amusing diversion—a way to keep his parents content that he dutifully searched for a wife—that is, until Miss Rossington's true nature emerged. She'd fully exposed herself this evening, and her revelation had relegated her to an unsuitable.

"Oh." Olivia fiddled with the elaborate pendant nestled above her décolletage.

Envy seized him. He would like to take the pendant's hallowed place.

The matching ruby bracelet on her wrist sparkled in the muted light when she waved her hand. "And I suppose, as their son, you must do your *duty*?"

He hid a delighted smile.

Yes. Jealousy most definitely tinged her husky voice, though she attempted to disguise it with sarcasm. He quite enjoyed the notion she was jealous. It meant she still cared.

Rolling his head, he nodded once and grinned. "I like to think I'm a very dutiful son."

Actually, except for a couple years before meeting Olivia when he had sowed his wild oats, he had been the epitome of propriety. Not only did his parents insist upon it, he'd found he wasn't cut out to be a man about town. The drinking, whoring, gambling—all favorite pastimes of many of the *ton's* privileged—held little appeal for him. Though hopelessly unpopular with the elite set, he rather favored a quiet life with one woman in his bed. Olivia.

She cocked her head, one earring swinging with the action. "Ah, yet you expected me to forsake my duty as an obedient daughter and leave my father?"

Her words ripped apart Allen's attempt at light-heartedness. Damn, this wasn't the path he'd intended their conversation to take. Olivia had neatly turned the tables on him.

"Did it ever occur to you that demanding we elope at once scared and unnerved me?" She pressed her palm to her chest, her features taut. "Every bit as much as Father announcing we were off to the Caribbean in two days' time? Both situations frightened the living daylights out of me."

Her revelation rendered Allen mute. Her situation had been wholly impossible, made worse by his juvenile ultimatum.

"Papa's health had deteriorated since Mama died." Tucking a loose tendril behind her ear, Olivia inhaled deeply, as if struggling for control. She sent a furtive look to the terrace, no doubt worried about her reputation. "Defying Papa might have killed him. How could I have lived with myself then?"

Her eyes glistened suspiciously once more.

Whirling away, she wandered to a row of rosebushes edging another neat path. "You hadn't even asked Papa for my hand yet. He knew nothing of your intentions."

"We had only known each other a fortnight, Livy." Allen rubbed his nape before folding his arms. "I doubt your father would have received my request with any enthusiasm."

You could have made the effort, dolt.

"I'm not sure it would have made a difference in any event." She shrugged and offered a rueful tilt of her plump lips as she removed one glove. "My father was impetuous and disinclined to think about how his impromptu decisions might affect others. I've always suspected he didn't want me to ever wed."

Allen canted his head again. "And you truly knew nothing of his intentions? To pack you off to the Caribbean with no warning?" He gestured in the air. "I'm sure you can understand why I might find that hard to believe."

"Allen, you come from a stable home. You know nothing of living with a parent who acted on the slightest whim. It wasn't unusual for Papa to pack us up and cart the family off to some absurd location when he became obsessed with another peculiar notion. Bradford was spared somewhat when he went off to university. I've often wondered if the only reason he came back home when he finished was to act as a buffer and protect me."

Olivia bent and sniffed a creamy rose then released a small cry of pain. Thrusting her finger into her mouth, she sucked the scarlet droplet from the tip where a thorn had scratched her.

At the sensual sight, Allen's throat went dry as a more erotic image leaped to mind.

Egads, she's hurt, and I'm envisioning lewd acts.

After a moment, Olivia regained her composure. After tugging on her glove once more, she continued her hesitant exploration of the flowers.

"Why Papa kept the news of our departure a secret is anyone's guess. He was always been a bit eccentric and reclusive. After Mama's death, he became more so. And at times—I'm ashamed to admit—quite addlebrained, especially as he aged."

Another wave of guilt hammered Allen. Her father

was ailing and, apparently, dicked in the nob, to boot. "I had no idea."

Stroking a velvety petal, she lifted a shoulder. "No one did. One doesn't discuss such delicate matters. It wasn't until after we'd arrived in Barbados that Papa confessed his physician had recommended a change of climate in order to extend his life. The milder tropical weather was supposed to improve both his health and his doldrums."

Remorse crushed Allen's chest. He hadn't known any of this, though it didn't excuse his brash behavior. He'd wager his inheritance that after his harsh ultimatum, Olivia's pride had kept her from telling him. Tarring and feathering was too merciful for him. His handling of the whole affair bordered on—no, *was* completely—despicable.

Striving for control, Allen tilted his head skyward and sucked in a steadying breath. "How long have you been in England?"

He lowered his eyes, unable to keep his gaze from feasting on her in the soft light. He needed to soothe her pain, to make amends for the hurt he'd caused. He yearned to hold her in his arms, as he had ached to do every day while she had been away.

"Just over a week." Head bowed, she folded her hands before her. "Bradford and I are staying with the duchess until other arrangements can be made. Our uncle let the Mayfair house and Bradford's never been fond of it so we're seeking accommodations elsewhere."

She's been back a week and made no effort to contact me?

"Three years, Olivia. You asked me to wait one, but you've been gone three years." Allen winced at the pain he heard in his voice.

Her gaze collided with his. Regret and something else flashed in the azure depths.

"I intended to return after a year. We all did, but Papa had apoplexy four months after we arrived. He never fully recovered, and the physician advised us travel was out of the question." Her eyes shone glassy with tears. "He said it would kill Papa."

"You never wrote." Allen wandered to the flower beds to stand beside her. She was so close, only a handbreadth away, yet a yawning abyss of unbridgeable misunderstanding lay between them.

Olivia touched another rose. "And what would I have said? You made your position very clear. You also said you wouldn't wait for me."

Each bitter truth impaled him. "You might have told me of your father's ill health."

"To what purpose?" She cast him a sidelong look.

He snapped a rose's stem then offered it to her.

"I would have known why you didn't return." *To me,* he ached to add.

"I thought you had come to hate me, Allen."

Intelligence, wit, and a polite
smile are a lady's greatest weapons.
~*A Lady's Guide to Proper Comportment*

7

Accepting the scarlet rose, Olivia solemnly faced Allen. Even in the dim light, with only moonbeams and the glow from the house's windows, she glimpsed a trace of vulnerability in his turned down mouth and hooded gaze.

She had never been able to hide her emotions from him. What did she have to lose by being completely candid now? Not a blasted thing. After tonight, she would likely never see him again. She lifted the flower to her nose. Shutting her eyes, she sniffed deeply.

He'd given her a red rose. Did he know they symbolized love? Likely not. Purely chance he had selected that color of bloom. Foolish of her to wish the gesture meant more.

"I was so young—having just seen my eighteenth birthday the month before—and when you suggested we run away to marry that night, I panicked." She waved her hand back and forth. "Everything happened so fast between us."

He scowled, kicking at a stone lying on the grass. "Our love was real. Don't tell me it wasn't."

Olivia nodded, and another curl slid free to tease her ear. Why bother to put her hair up at all?

"Yes, I know it is ... was." She stumbled over her words, but recovered, her voice softening. "I've never doubted it for a moment."

He fingered a fragile petal. "Then why did you leave?"

"Why did you let me go?" She peered into his unfathomable eyes.

If he had only made some sort of effort, had come to her house or the ship, done anything to prevent her from leaving, her resolve would have melted as rapidly as sugar in hot tea.

The Lady's Guide to Proper Comportment says a

lady never complains or criticizes—

Do hush, Mama.

Rubbing his thumb and forefinger together, Allen gazed off into space for an extended moment. The quiet hum of the guests on the terrace, the faint strains of the orchestra, and an occasional cricket's rasping song interrupted his weighty silence.

"My devilish pride," he finally murmured, splaying his fingers through his hair, leaving several tufts standing straight up. If his valet saw his destroyed handiwork, he would gnaw Allen's hairbrush to a nub. "I've always been too prideful. Arrogant some might say. Definitely privileged, and I seldom don't get what I want."

Allen's honest confession startled her, and Olivia dared to harbor the tiniest bit of optimism.

Grinning sheepishly, he rolled a shoulder. "I couldn't credit that you would leave me, that you expected me to wait a year for your return. I desired you then, and I acted the part of an intractable bratling."

"You broke my heart." Utterly shattered it was more apt.

He hadn't indicated he still cared for her, only that he had been as hurt as she. A breeze wafted past, and she crossed her arms, suddenly chilled. She must return inside soon, else Aunt Muriel and Bradford would become worried, not to mention the gossip Olivia and Allen's extended stay outdoors would ignite. "Fearing your scorn, I didn't dare reach out to you afterward. I have my pride too."

"I know, and I'm remorseful beyond words."

Stepping nearer, he took her hand in his. With his other, he lifted her chin until their eyes met. "Can you forgive me? Please? Might we begin again and take our time this go round?" He playfully tugged one of the escaped curls then caressed her cheek with his forefinger. "I promise not to be demanding and to always consider your feelings and needs. I beg you, give me another chance."

Blinking back tears of joy, Olivia swallowed the lump of emotion choking her. Even when the carriage had rattled to a stop before the mansion, she couldn't have imagined this most welcome turn of events. She nodded as one tear spilled from the corner of her eye.

Allen caught it with his forefinger. "I never want to make you cry again, Livy. A least not from sorrow I caused. Happiness or passion, yes, but never ... never tears of unhappiness again."

He kissed her forehead before resting his against hers.

They were probably being observed, and the tattlemongers would be flapping their tongues until next Season, but she didn't care. In fact, Olivia wouldn't be surprised if Aunt Muriel—silently cheering, and clapping, and congratulating herself soundly for contriving this whole wonderful evening—wasn't lurking somewhere nearby, perhaps in those bushes just there, watching everything that transpired between Allen and her.

"I never stopped loving you." He kissed Olivia's nose. "Not for a single moment. When you left, the light went out of my life. I never wanted to smile again, and I cursed the sun for rising each day. I knew my selfishness and inconsideration had cost me the one thing that mattered most. You."

"Oh, Allen." She traced his jaw with her fingertips. "If only we had talked this through, this misunderstanding wouldn't have kept us apart all this time. Promise me we'll always be able to tell the other anything, and that we'll listen before ever jumping to conclusions or acting rashly again."

"Always." He grasped her hand and pressed a hot kiss into her palm. The heat of his lips burned through the fabric of her glove, sending delicious frissons spiraling outward. "Tell me you love me still, Livy. That there's a morsel of hope for us."

"Yes." She grinned and nodded. More curls sprang free. She didn't care. "I do love you."

He released a long breath, as if he had been afraid of her response. "Will you marry me? Not right away. We can wait if you wish. I won't rush you. I know I asked you before, but I want to go about it properly this time."

"Of course I will." She toyed with his jacket's lapel, giving him a coy smile. "Then you'll ask Bradford—?"

"Ask Bradford what?"

She whipped around to see her brother standing

behind them. So caught up in the magical moment with Allen, she hadn't heard him approach. From the nonplussed expression on Allen's face, he hadn't either.

"Ask me what?" Bradford repeated, curiosity glinting in his eyes as he came nearer.

Allen stood taller and met his gaze straight on. "For your sister's hand in marriage."

Bradford's face broke into an immense grin, and he clapped his hands.

"Thank God. I had no idea what I was going to do with her if you two didn't reconcile." He planted his hands on his hips. "She has been in the doldrums for months and months, a regular Friday face, I tell you, scarcely cracking a smile during her fit of the blue devils and—"

Olivia whacked his arm with her fan. "That's enough, Brady. Say another word, and I shall not invite you to the wedding."

Revealing his perfect white teeth, Allen returned Bradford's silly grin. "Then we have your approval?"

"I'll say." Bradford chuckled heartily while pumping Allen's hand "My approval, consent, permission, blessing—"

"Bradford," Olivia warned. Must he carry on so? She hadn't been so awful, had she?

His eyes widened. "By George, I'll even pay for a special license, and we can have the deed done tomorrow."

"Not so fast, brother dear, else I may take offense at your eagerness to be rid of me." Olivia swung her amused gaze to Allen. "I should like a short courtship, but I would also like a wedding. Aunt Muriel will insist upon it, in any case."

Allen raised her hand to his lips. "Whatever you wish, sweetheart. I'm eager to make you my bride, but won't rush you. I'm just as certain my mother will want an elaborate showing too." He winked. "I think it may be dangerous to allow the duchess and my mother to put their heads together. We might very well end up with the wedding of the decade."

Olivia laughed. "Yes, Aunt Muriel is a force to contend with."

"There you are, Allen, my dear." Miss Rossington glided across the lawn.

A KISS FOR A ROGUE

Allen?

Only intimate acquaintances addressed one another by their first names, and unless betrothed to a gentleman, a young lady never did so in public. And she most certainly did not call him her dear.

A Lady's Guide to Proper Comportment, page thirty-six.

Her fine brow puckered in puzzlement, Miss Rossington looked between Allen and Olivia then turned her attention to Bradford, eyeing him like a delicious pastry she would like to savor. Or gobble up, rather. She batted her eyelashes and licked her lips provocatively.

Brazen as an east end bit of muslin.

"Whatever is going on?" She lowered her voice to a sultry whisper, her wanton wiles in full play.

Wasted on Bradford. He might like dampened gowns and appreciate a beautiful face and form, but he couldn't abide fast women, and Miss Rossington would make it round the racetrack swifter than The Derby's prime blood.

Olivia couldn't suppress her pleased smile as Allen wrapped a muscled arm about her waist and tucked her to his side, even if his actions were outside of acceptable.

"Miss Kingsley has just done me the greatest honor by consenting to become my wife."

"What?" Miss Rossington, sounding is if she had gargled gravel, blanched and clutched her throat. "Your ... your *wife*?"

"Indeed. I told you she was the woman I almost married." He gave Olivia's waist a squeeze. "Well, now I'm beyond blessed to say that dream will at last come to pass."

Miss Rossington stomped toward Allen, her countenance contorted in rage. "You damned churl, toying with my affections. Do you know how many men's address I refused?"

Allen lifted a brow. "We both know that's utter gammon. An alley cat has more discretion."

The blonde sputtered and choked, daggers shooting from her eyes. She whipped her arm back as if to strike Allen. "Why you—"

Bradford swiftly stepped forward and snared her

hand.

"I wouldn't. Do you truly want those denizens witnessing you acting the part of a shrew?" He thrust his chin toward the terrace. "I assure you, a dead codfish, green and rotting, has a greater chance of finding a husband amongst the *haute ton* than you do if you strike the son of a peer."

Yanking her hand from his, Miss Rossington turned on Allen. "You bloody bastard."

The curl of his lips simultaneously expressed his scorn and amusement.

Teeth clenched and seething with rage, she glared at Bradford then Olivia. "Damn you all to the ninth circle of hell."

Hiking her gown to mid-calf, Miss Rossington spun on her satin slippered heel. She proceeded to stomp her way back to the house, muttering additional foul oaths a woman of gentle breeding should never have let pass her lips.

Page nineteen, paragraph two.

A form separated from the shadows on one side of the French windows.

Olivia blinked in disbelief as Aunt Muriel emerged from behind the drapes. Olivia would wager the Prussian jewels she wore, her aunt had been watching the whole while.

Aunt Muriel lifted her nose and pulled her skirts aside as Miss Rossington tramped into the house. Then with a little wave at Olivia, Aunt Muriel bolted out of sight. Likely to apprise the Wimpletons of what she had witnessed.

The adorable sneak.

"It seems we've drawn a crowd." Chagrin heated Olivia's cheeks as she canted her head slightly in the terrace's direction. At least a score of guests mingled about the porch, their rapt attention focused on the trio left standing on the grass.

Dash it all. Allen hadn't wanted additional fodder for le bon ton's gossipmongers.

A roguish glint entered his eyes. "Let's make it worth their while, shall we, darling?"

A lady never participates in public shows of affection.

Olivia cast a glance heavenward.

Then I guess I'm not a lady, Mama.

She didn't resist when Allen drew her into his embrace, although she cast her brother a hesitant look.

Bradford winked. "Please do, Wimpleton. Give the chinwags something to babble about. Make it something quite spectacular, will you? Something scandalous to keep their forked tongues flapping for a good long while."

With a smart salute, he turned his back on them and, whistling a jaunty tune, strolled along the path wending into the garden's depths.

Bradford was proving to be every bit as indecorous as their aunt.

Olivia inclined her head and eyed Allen. "Well? What outrageousness do you have in mind?"

"A kiss, perhaps?" He ran his thumb across her lower lip.

Olivia quite liked this rakish side of him. "Oh, yes."

Allen took another step closer, and his thighs pressed against hers, their chests colliding.

Winding her arms around his neck, she raised her

mouth in invitation.

A scandalized voice carried across the expanse. "Do you see that? They're kissing. Right there on the lawn. In full view of all."

"Yes. It's utterly lovely, isn't it?" Aunt Muriel's delighted laugh filled the night air.

Allen dipped his dark head until their lips were a hair's breadth apart. "A kiss for Miss Kingsley?"

"Perfect." Olivia smiled as his mouth claimed hers.

Epilogue

Wyndleyford House
September 1818

"Do finish up, Olivia darling. We'll be late."

Allen lounged against the bedpost, looking irresistibly dashing as he watched Olivia's last-minute fussing. His pristine cravat was tied in another new, complicated knot, and his waistcoat matched his green eyes to perfection. However, it was the gleam of male satisfaction in his jungle gaze that sent her pulse cavorting again.

"It's not my fault you decided to exercise your husbandly rights just as I exited my bath."

Olivia gave him a playful pout as she deliberately applied perfume to her cleavage. That quite drove him mad. She touched the emeralds at her throat. He had placed them there just before they'd spent a blissful half an hour abed. "My *toilette* would have been completed long ago."

"I didn't hear you complaining overly much." Allen straightened and after adjusting his jacket sleeves, crossed the room, his long-legged strides covering the distance in short order. He bent and kissed her bare shoulder. "I knew the Wimpleton emeralds would look exquisite on you."

"They are stunning. Thank you." She turned her head up for a kiss. The scorching meeting of their mouths had her considering an even tardier arrival to her new in-laws' anniversary celebration. "I'm honored to wear them to the festivities tonight."

"It's our anniversary too, love. One month today, Mrs. Wimpleton. Slowest three months of my life, waiting to make you my bride."

She grinned. "I told you it was dangerous to let my aunt and your mother help plan our wedding. I about tripped over my dress when I saw Prinny sitting in a front pew."

"You and I both. I'd never seen a man attired completely in that shade of pink before. Looked rather like an enormous, glittery salmon." Allen withdrew a bracelet from his pocket then lifted her hand.

"More?" Olivia shook her head. "It's magnificent but, you know, I'm not a woman who requires jewels. I have all I ever wanted."

He settled it around her wrist and set the clasp. "Would you deny me my pleasure?"

Quirking her brow, she gave him an impish smile. "When have I *ever* denied you your pleasure?"

With a mock growl, he pulled her to her feet. Swinging her into his embrace, he plundered her mouth.

A scratching at the door interrupted the kiss. "Sir, madam, everyone has arrived."

"I suppose we must put in an appearance." Allen sighed and leaned away, acting put-upon.

Giggling, Olivia collected her shawl and fan. "Of course we must. Your sister and my brother are below with their spouses. Your parents must host more balls. Three weddings came about as a result of that one in May."

"I do believe that rout set a record." He chuckled and scratched his nose. At the door he caught her arm.

"Have I told you that I love you today, Mrs. Wimpleton?"

She touched his face. "Yes, but I shall never tire of hearing it."

He dropped a kiss onto her forehead. "And I promise I shall never tire of saying it."

About the Author

USA Today Bestselling, award-winning author COLLETTE CAMERON® scribbles Scottish and Regency historicals featuring dashing rogues and scoundrels and the intrepid damsels who re-form them. Blessed with an overactive and witty muse that won't stop whispering new romantic romps in her ear, she's lived in Oregon her entire life, though she dreams of living in Scotland part-time. A self-confessed Cadbury chocoholic, you'll always find a dash of inspiration and a pinch of humor in her sweet-to-spicy timeless romances®.

Explore **Collette's worlds** at
www.collettecameron.com!

Join her **VIP Reader Club** and **FREE newsletter**.
Giggles guaranteed!

FREE BOOK: Join Collette's The Regency Rose® VIP Reader Club to get updates on book releases, cover reveals, contests and giveaways she reserves exclusively for email and newsletter followers. Also, any deals, sales, or special promotions are offered to club members first. She will not share your name or email, nor will she spam you.

http://bit.ly/TheRegencyRoseGift

From the Desk of Collette Cameron

Dearest Reader,

A Kiss for a Rogue was inspired by a scene in ***Triumph and Treasure*** that mentions the Wimpletons' ball. I had so much fun writing the story, I decided to create a new novella series featuring waltzes and rogues. Hence, The Honorable Rogues® series was born.

Readers said they wanted more time with Olivia and Allen, and that's why I expanded their story in this second edition. I'm truly delighted you chose to read ***A Kiss for a Rogue***, and I hope it capitated you enough to take a peek at the other books in the series.

Please consider telling other readers why you enjoyed the book by reviewing on the site where you purchased it. Not only do I truly want to hear your thoughts, reviews are crucial for an author to succeed. **Even if you only leave a line or two, I'd very much appreciate it.**

So, with that I'll leave you.

Here's wishing you many happy hours of reading, more happily ever afters than you can possibly enjoy in a lifetime, and abundant blessings to you and your loved-ones.

Collette Cameron

A Bride for a Rogue

The Honorable Rogues®, Book Two

Formerly titled Bride of Falcon

She can't forget the past. He can't face the future. Until fate intervenes one night.

Many years ago, Ivonne Wimpleton loved Chancy Faulkenhurst and hoped to marry him. Then one day, without any explanation, he sailed to India. Now, after five unsuccessful Seasons and a riding accident that left her with a slight limp, her only suitors are fortune-hunters and degenerates. Just as Ivy's resigned herself to spinsterhood, Chance unexpectedly returns.

Upon returning to England, Chance is disillusioned, disfigured, and emotionally scarred, but his love for Ivy remains is strong. However, he's failed to acquire the fortune he sought in order to earn permission to marry her. When he discovers Ivy's being forced to wed to prevent a scandalous secret from being revealed, he's determined to make her his bride.

Except, believing Chance made no effort to contact her all those years, Ivy's furious with him. What's more, in his absence, his father arranged a profitable marriage for Chance. As he battles his own inner demons, he must convince Ivy to risk loving him again. But will their parents' interference jeopardize Chance and Ivy's happiness once more?

Excerpt

Enjoy the first chapter of

A Bride for a Rogue

The Honorable Rogues™, Book Two

1

London, England, Late May, 1818

"There you are, Miss Wimpleton."

Ivonne Wimpleton whipped her gaze to Captain Melvin Kirkpatrick. Groaning in frustration, she snapped her fan closed, prepared to use the frilly accessory to give him a good poke or two, if necessary.

Fiend seize it. What is he doing here?

He must have arrived after she ventured outdoors.

She'd specifically asked Mother not to invite him

tonight. Somehow, the bore had finagled an invitation to accompany another guest. Ivonne had hoped he'd finally sailed for Africa and wouldn't impose his unwelcome presence on her for six blessed months or more.

He staggered toward her secluded bench on the side terrace, a drunken smile skewing his mouth.

She shot to her feet, searching for a means to avoid him. The only possibility lay in the narrow stairway descending to the manicured garden where an occasional colored lantern glowed. Ivonne strode toward her salvation at a near run.

Captain Kirkpatrick caught her arm and pinned her against the balustrade with his great weight. Her fan fell, clattering to the flagstone.

Straining against him, Ivonne fought to breathe and gagged. Did the man ever bathe?

"What audacity. Unhand me, sir!"

He shook his head. Excitement glimmered in his glassy eyes. "I think not. You've played the reluctant miss long enough. It's time you tasted what our married life will be like."

A BRIDE FOR A ROGUE Excerpt

"Are you dicked in the nob?" Though no match for his strength, Ivonne still fought to break free. As she struggled, her hair pins came loose and scattered onto the stones. "I. Am. Not. Marrying. You."

He tightened his clasp, and she winced as he held her arms in a bruising grip.

"I prefer blondes with blue eyes, but I cannot complain about your curves." Leering at her bosom, Captain Kirkpatrick licked his lips. He pawed her breast with one beefy hand as his other gripped her head in an attempt to steal a kiss.

His foul breath assailed Ivonne, sending her stomach pitching at the stench of strong spirits and onions. Intent on screaming like a banshee, she opened her mouth and sucked in a huge breath.

A chortling foursome of gentlemen burst through the French windows onto the other side of the terrace. Their sudden appearance rescued her from the captain's lewd groping. Panting heavily, his bushy red eyebrows scrunched together, he released her and scowled at her brother, Allen, Lords Sethwick and Luxmoore, and the Duke of Harcourt.

A pity the new arrivals weren't her twin cousins, Edwina and Edward. They would come to her aid and not breathe a word of the untoward situation. However, if Allen spied her in Captain Kirkpatrick's company, there would be the devil to pay.

Ivonne tried to blend into the manor's shadow, but the sea captain's stout form obstructed her. Her brother had warned the widower away from her once already. If he suspected the captain dared lay a hand on her, Allen would call him out. A dab hand at pistols—all firearms, for that matter—Captain Kirkpatrick might wound, or, heaven forbid, kill dear Allen.

She shuddered. It must not come to that. She peeked at the captain from beneath her lashes. More than a trifle disguised, his drunken focus remained on the other men. Ivonne seized the moment. Without hesitation, she kneed him in the ballocks with her good leg and gave him a mighty shove.

Bent double and growling in fury, he stumbled backward, clutching his groin.

Ignoring his gasps of pain and vile curses, she edged away. With one eye on the laughing quartet, she crept down the stairs. Once out of their view, she flew across the lawn as rapidly as her injured leg would allow. She'd broken the limb in two places in a riding accident three years ago. The leg pained her on occasion, and she endured a permanent, though slight, limp made worse by overexertion.

She darted behind a tall rose-covered trellis. In her haste, the ball gown's black net overskirt caught on a thorn-laden cane. Breathing labored and leg throbbing, she halted just inside the alcove and gave the skirt a gentle tug.

Dash it all. Stuck fast.

She sent a frantic glance along the footpath.

A twig snapped. Had Captain Kirkpatrick followed her?

A jolt of fright raised the hairs on her arms and stole her breath. Did she dare step outside the arbor and release the material? Would he see her if she did? She couldn't move farther into the enclosure, though if she remained here, she risked almost certain discovery.

A sleepy dove cooed from somewhere in the garden's trees. The night's festivities had no doubt disturbed its slumber.

Ivonne peered through the lattice slats.

Where was he?

With her forefinger, she nudged a couple of leaves aside. Her white gloves stood out, a stark contrast against the plants. Oh, to have the mythical mantel of Arthur in Cornwall and be invisible.

A soft wind wafted through her hiding place and rustled the leaves overhead. Several spun lazily to the ground. Guests' laughter and the lilting strains of the orchestra floated through the beveled French windows and carried to her on the mild breeze.

What possessed her to give into the impulse to venture outside alone and catch some air?

Because you dislike balls, gentlemen treating you as if you're beneath their touch, and all the pretentious nastiness that's generally present when the denizens of High Society gather.

Though only May, the crush of the crowd inside the mansion caused the temperature to rise uncomfortably. The heat, mixed with cloying perfumes, less-than-fresh clothing, the aroma of dozens of beeswax candles, and the occasional unbathed body, made her head ache and stomach queasy.

She'd sought a secluded niche on the side terrace to recover. Unfortunately, Captain Kirkpatrick, deep in his cups, found her there. Much like the shaggy bull he resembled, he'd stalked her at every social gathering.

A more off-putting man she'd never met.

Ivonne turned sideways and hoped the vines' thick cover concealed her. If fear had a scent, the captain's bulbous nose would lead him straight to her. Heavy footfalls crunched upon the gravel not more than a yard away. She closed her eyes as her heart lurched to her throat. Thank God she hadn't tried to detach her gown. He'd have been on her like dense winter fog on the River Thames.

"Miss Wimpleton, you saucy minx, where are you?"

A low, suggestive chuckle followed. "I do like a spirited gel in my bed. I do, indeed."

Ivonne's eyes popped open. Captain Kirkpatrick's gloating singsong whisper sent a shiver of loathing the length of her spine. She bit her lower lip, afraid to exhale lest he detect her presence.

He advanced another foot, pausing before the lattice.

She clenched her jaw and shut her eyes.

He stood so close, the noxious mixture of his dinner, pungent cologne, and sweat assaulted her nose. Hot bile rose to her throat, and she swallowed against the burning. Her nose twitched. Flaring her nostrils, she fought to suppress a sneeze.

If he discovered her hidden within the nook, there'd be no escaping the man's amorous attentions. He might claim to prefer blondes, but he'd become bolder each time she encountered him. Given the opportunity, God alone knew what the foxed knave might try in this private bower. Look what he'd attempted on the veranda in full view of anyone who might have come along.

Holding her breath, she pursed her lips.

Do not sneeze.

The captain planted his hands on his ample hips and scanned the shrubberies. He turned in a slow circle. The straining gold buttons of his black tailcoat gleamed in the moonbeams bathing the path. He withdrew a silver flask from his pocket, and after a furtive glance around, took a couple of healthy gulps.

"Where are you? Come out, my sweet." He belched and returned the flask to his pocket. "No need to be coy. I have something of importance to ask you."

Precisely why Ivonne huddled like a timid mouse amongst the foliage outside her parents' mansion. In the past two months, he'd asked the same question thrice before. Her firm "No" each time hadn't deterred him in the least. In fact, her reluctance appeared to make the stocky widower more determined to win her hand.

Grimacing and cautious to keep her gown from rustling, she shifted her weight to her good leg.

Ah, much better.

Wisteria and salmon-colored climbing roses concealed the garden nook. Her favorite hideaway, normally, she would have relished the fragrant air surrounding her. Tonight, however, she could only be grateful the roses' scent masked her perfume and hadn't produced a fit of sneezing.

Ivonne swallowed against the tickle teasing her throat. If only she dared pinch her nostrils. She mustn't. Her gloves against the verdant leaves might give her away. Yearning to slip into one of the nook's inky corners, she yanked her skirt again. The fabric didn't budge.

Captain Kirkpatrick swung his dark gaze to the trellis.

A Rogue's Scandalous Wish
The Honorable Rogues®, Book Three

Formerly titled Her Scandalous Wish

**A marriage offered out of obligation…
…an acceptance compelled by desperation.**

At the urging of her dying brother, Philomena Pomfrett reluctantly agrees to attend a London Season. If she fails to acquire a husband, her future is perilous. Betrayed once by Bradford, Viscount Kingsley, as well as scarred from a horrific fire, Philomena entertains no notions of a love-match. Hers will be a marriage of convenience. *If* she can find man who will have her.

When the woman he loves dies, Bradford leaves England and its painful memories behind. After a three-year absence, he returns home but doesn't recognize his first love when he stumbles upon her hiding in a shadowy arbor during a ball. Something about the mysterious woman enthralls him, and he steals a moonlit kiss. Caught in the act by Philomena's brother, Bradford is issued an ultimatum—a duel or marry her.

Bradford refuses to duel with a gravely-ill man and offers marriage. But Philomena rejects his half-hearted proposal, convinced he'd grow to despise her when he sees her disfiguring scars. Then her brother collapses, and frantic to provide the medical care he needs, she's faced with marrying a man who deserted her once already.

To Capture a Rogue's Heart

The Honorable Rogues®, Book Four

Formerly titled To Tame a Scoundrel's Heart

**He recruited her to help him find a wife...
...and discovered she was the perfect candidate.**

Her betrothed cheated on her.
Katrina Needham intended to marry her beloved major and live happily-ever-after—until he's seen with another woman. Distraught, and needing a distraction, she agrees to assist the rugged, and dangerously handsome Captain Dominic St. Monté find a wife. So why does she find herself entertaining romantic notions about the privateer turned duke?

He believed he was illegitimate.
When Nic unexpectedly inherits a dukedom and the care of his young sisters, he reluctantly decides he must marry. Afterward, if his new duchess is willing, he hopes to return to the sea-faring life he craves part-time. If she doesn't agree, he'll have no choice but to give up the sea forever.

Will they forsake everything for each other?
Nic soon realizes Katrina possesses every characteristic he seeks in a duchess. The more time he spends with the vivacious beauty, the more enamored he becomes. Still, he cannot ask for her hand. Not only is she still officially promised to another, she has absolutely no interest in becoming a duchess, much less a privateer's wife.

Can Nic and Katrina relinquish their carefully planned futures and trust love to guide them?

The Rogue and the Wallflower

The Honorable Rogues®, Book Five

Formerly titled The Wallflower's Wicked Wager

He loved her beyond anything and everything—precisely why he must never marry her.

Love—sentimental drivel for weak, feckless fools.
Since an explosion ravaged Captain Morgan Le Draco's face and cost him his commission in the Royal Dragoons, he's fortified himself behind a rampart of cynicism and distrust. He's put aside all thoughts of marrying until he risks his life to save a drowning woman. At once, Morgan knows Shona's the balm for his tortured soul. But as a wealthy noblewoman, she's far above his humble station and can never be his.

Love—a treasured gift reserved for those beautiful of form and face.
Scorned and ridiculed most of her adult life, Shona Atterberry believes she's utterly undesirable and is reconciled to spinsterhood. She hides her spirited

temperament beneath a veneer of shyness. Despite how ill-suited they are, and innuendos that Captain Le Draco is a fortune-hunter, she cannot escape her growing fascination.

Two damaged souls searching for love.
Shona is goaded into placing a wicked wager. One that sets her upon a ruinous path and alienates the only man who might have ever loved her. Is true love enough to put their pasts behind them, to learn to trust, and to heal their wounded hearts.

The Earl and the Spinster

The Blue Rose Regency Romances:
The Culpepper Misses, Book One

Formerly titled Brooke: Wagers Gone Awry

**An angry earl. A desperate spinster.
A reckless wager.**

For five years, Brooke Culpepper has focused her energy on two things: keeping the struggling dairy farm that's her home operating and preventing her younger sister and cousins from starving. Then one day, a stern-faced stranger arrives at their doorstep and announces he's the dairy's new owner and plans on selling the farm. Though she's outraged, Brooke can't deny the Earl of Ravensdale makes her pulse race in the most disturbing way.

Heath is incensed to discover five women call the land he won at the gaming tables their home. He detests everything about the country and has no desire to own a smelly farm, even if one of the occupants is the most intelligent, entrancing woman he's ever met.

Desperate, pauper poor, and with nowhere to take her family, Brooke rashly proposes a wager. Heath's stakes? The farm. Hers? Her virtue. The land holds no interest for Heath, but he finds Brooke irresistible, and ignoring prudence as well as his sense of honor, he just as recklessly accepts her challenge.

In a winner-takes-all bet, will they both come to regret their impulsiveness, especially when love is at stake?

Excerpt

Enjoy the first chapter of
The Earl and the Spinster
The Blue Rose Regency Romances:
The Culpepper Misses, Book One

Even when most prudently considered,
and with the noblest of intentions, one who
wagers with chance oft finds oneself empty-handed.
~*Wisdom and Advice*
The Genteel Lady's Guide to Practical Living

1

Esherton Green,
Near Acton, Cheshire, England
Early April 1822

Was I born under an evil star or cursed from my first breath?

Brooke Culpepper suppressed the urge to shake her fist at the heavens and berate The Almighty aloud.

The devil boasted better luck than she. My God, now two *more* cows struggled to regain their strength?

She slid Richard Mabry, Esherton Green's steward-turned-overseer, a worried glance from beneath her lashes as she chewed her lower lip and paced before the unsatisfactory fire in the study's hearth. The soothing aroma of wood smoke, combined with linseed oil, old leather, and the faintest trace of Papa's pipe tobacco, bathed the room. The scents reminded her of happier times but did little to calm her frayed nerves.

Sensible gray woolen skirts swishing about her ankles, she whirled to make the return trip across the once-bright green and gold Axminster carpet, now so threadbare, the oak floor peeked through in numerous places. Her scuffed half-boots fared little better, and she hid a wince when the scrap of leather she'd used to cover the hole in her left sole this morning slipped loose again.

From his comfortable spot in a worn and faded wingback chair, Freddy, her aged Welsh corgi, observed her progress with soulful brown eyes, his muzzle propped on stubby paws. Two ancient tabbies lay curled so tightly together on the cracked leather sofa that determining where one ended and the other began was difficult.

What was she to do? Brooke clamped her lip harder and winced.

Should she venture to the barn to see the cows herself?

What good would that do? She knew little of doctoring cattle and so left the animals' care in Mr. Mabry's capable hands. Her strength lay in the financial administration of the dairy farm and her ability to stretch a shilling as thin as gossamer.

She cast a glance at the bay window and, despite the fire, rubbed her arms against the chill creeping along her spine. A frenzied wind whipped the lilac branches and scraped the rain-splattered panes. The tempest threatening since dawn had finally unleashed its full fury, and the fierce winds battering the house gave the day a peculiar, eerie feeling—as if portending something ominous.

At least Mabry and the other hands had managed

to get the cattle tucked away before the gale hit. The herd of fifty—no, sixty, counting the newborn calves—chewed their cud and weathered the storm inside the old, but sturdy, barns.

As she peered through the blurry pane, a shingle ripped loose from the farthest outbuilding—a retired stone dovecote. After the wind tossed the slat around for a few moments, the wood twirled to the ground, where it flipped end over end before wedging beneath a gangly shrub. Two more shingles hurled to the earth, this time from one of the barns.

Flimflam and goose-butt feathers.

Brooke tamped down a heavy sigh. Each structure on the estate, including the house, needed some sort of repair or replacement: roofs, shutters, stalls, floors, stairs, doors, siding...dozens of items required fixing, and she could seldom muster the funds to go about it properly.

"Another pair of cows struggling, you say, Mr. Mabry?"

Concern etched on his weathered features, Mabry wiped rain droplets from his face as water pooled at his muddy feet.

"Yes, Miss Brooke. The four calves born this mornin' fare well, but two of the cows, one a first-calf heifer, aren't standin' yet. And there's one weak from birthin' her calf yesterday." His troubled gaze strayed to the window. "Two more ladies are in labor. I best return to the barn. They seemed fine when I left, but I'd as soon be nearby."

Brooke nodded once. "Yes, we mustn't take any chances."

The herd had already been reduced to a minimum by disease and sales to make ends meet. She needed every shilling the cows' milk brought. Losing another, let alone two or three good breeders...

No, I won't think of it.

She stopped pacing and forced a cheerful smile. Nonetheless, from the skeptical look Mabry speedily masked, his thoughts ran parallel to hers—one reason she put her trust in the man. Honest and intelligent, he'd worked alongside her to restore the beleaguered herd and farm after Papa died. Their existence, their livelihood, everyone at Esherton's future depended on the estate flourishing once more.

"It's only been a few hours." *Almost nine, truth to tell.* Brooke scratched her temple. "Perhaps the ladies need a little more time to recover." *If they recovered.* "The calves are strong, aren't they?" *Please, God, they must be.* She held her breath, anticipating Mabry's response.

His countenance lightened and the merry sparkle returned to his eyes. "Aye, the mites are fine. Feedin' like they're hollow to their wee hooves."

Tension lessoned its ruthless grip, and hope peeked from beneath her vast mound of worries.

Six calves had been guaranteed in trade to her neighbor and fellow dairy farmer, Silas Huffington, for the grain and medicines he'd provided to see Esherton Green's herd through last winter. Brooke didn't have the means to pay him if the calves didn't survive—though the old reprobate had hinted he'd make her a deal of a much less respectable nature if she ran short of cattle with which to barter. Each pence she'd stashed away—groat by miserable groat, these past four years—lay in the hidden drawer of Papa's desk and must go to purchase a bull.

Wisdom had decreed replacing Old Buford two years ago but, short on funds, she'd waited until it was too late. His heart had stopped while he performed the duties expected of a breeding bull. Not the worst way to cock up one's toes...er, hooves, but she'd counted on him siring at least two-score calves this season and wagered everything on the calving this year and next. The poor brute had expired before he'd completed the job.

Her thoughts careened around inside her skull. Without a bull, she would lose everything.

My home, care of my sister and cousins, my reasons for existing.

She squared her shoulders, resolution strengthening her. She still retained the Culpepper sapphire parure set. If all else failed, she would pawn the jewelry. She'd planned on using the money from the gems' sale to bestow small marriage settlements on the girls. Still, pawning the set was a price worth paying to keep her family at Esherton Green, even if it meant that any chance of her sister and three cousins securing a decent match would evaporate faster than a dab of milk on a hot cook stove. Good standing and breeding meant little if one's fortune proved meaner than a churchyard beggar's.

"How's the big bull calf that came breech on Sunday?" Brooke tossed the question over her shoulder as she poked the fire and encouraged the blaze to burn hotter. After setting the tool aside, she faced the overseer.

"Greediest of the lot." Mabry laughed and slapped his thigh. "Quite the appetite he has, and friendly as our Freddy there. Likes his ears scratched too."

Brooke chuckled and ran her hand across Freddy's spine. The dog wiggled in excitement and stuck his rear legs straight out behind him, gazing at her in adoration. In his youth, he'd been an excellent cattle herder. Now he'd gone fat and arthritic, his sweet face gray to his eyebrows. On occasion, he still dashed after the cattle, the instinctive drive to herd deep in the marrow of his bones.

Another shudder shook her. Why was she so blasted cold today? She relented and placed a good-

THE EARL AND THE SPINSTER Excerpt

sized log atop the others. The feeble flames hissed and spat before greedily engulfing the new addition. Lord, she prayed she wasn't ailing. She simply couldn't afford to become ill.

A scratching at the door barely preceded the entrance of Duffen bearing a tea service. "Gotten to where a man cannot find a quiet corner to shut his eyes for a blink or two anymore."

Shuffling into the room, he yawned and revealed how few teeth remained in his mouth. One sock sagged around his ankle, his grizzled hair poked every which way, and his shirttail hung askew. Typical Duffen.

"Devil's day, it is." He scowled in the window's direction, his mouth pressed into a grim line. "Mark my words, trouble's afoot."

Not quite a butler, but certainly more than a simple retainer, the man, now hunched from age, had been a fixture at Esherton Green Brooke's entire life. He loved the place as much as, if not more than, she, and she couldn't afford to hire a servant to replace him. A light purse had forced Brooke to let the household staff go when Papa died. The cook, Mrs. Jennings, Duffen, and Flora, a maid-of-all-work, had stayed on. However, they received no salaries—only room and board.

The income from the dairy scarcely permitted Brooke to retain a few milkmaids and stable hands, yet not once had she heard a whispered complaint from anyone.

Everybody, including Brooke, her sister, Brette, and their cousins—Blythe, and the twins, Blaike and Blaire—did their part to keep the farm operating at a profit. A meager profit, particularly as, for the past five years, Esherton Green's legal heir, Sheridan Gainsborough, had received half the proceeds. In return, he permitted Brooke and the girls to reside there. He'd also been appointed their guardian. But, from his silence and failure to visit the farm, he seemed perfectly content to let her carry on as provider and caretaker.

"Ridiculous law. Only the next male in line can inherit," she muttered.

Especially when he proved a disinterested bore. Papa had thought so too, but the choice hadn't been his to make. If only she could keep the funds she sent to Sheridan each quarter, Brooke could make something of Esherton and secure her sister and cousins' futures too.

If wishes were gold pieces, I'd be rich indeed.

Brooke sneezed then sneezed again. Dash it all. A cold?

The fresh log snapped loudly, and Brooke started. The blaze's heat had failed to warm her opinion of her second cousin. She hadn't met him and lacked a personal notion of his character, but Papa had hinted that Sheridan was a scallywag and possessed unsavory habits.

A greedy sot, too.

The one time her quarterly remittance had been late, because Brooke had taken a tumble and broken her arm, he'd written a disagreeable letter demanding his money.

His money, indeed.

Sheridan had threatened to sell Esherton Green's acreage and turn her and the foursome onto the street if she ever delayed payment again.

A ruckus beyond the entrance announced the girls' arrival. Laughing and chatting, the blond quartet billowed into the room. Their gowns, several seasons out of fashion, in no way detracted from their charm, and pride swelled in Brooke's heart. Lovely, both in countenance and disposition, and the dears worked hard too.

"Duffen says we're to have tea in here today." Attired in a Pomona green gown too short for her tall frame, Blaike plopped on to the sofa. Her twin, Blaire, wearing a similar dress in dark rose and equally inadequate in length, flopped beside her.

Each girl scooped a drowsy cat into her lap. The cats' wiry whiskers twitched, and they blinked their sleepy amber eyes a few times before closing them once more as the low rumble of contented purrs filled the room.

"Yes, I didn't think we needed to light a fire in the drawing room when this one will suffice." As things stood, too little coal and seasoned firewood remained to see them comfortably until summer.

Brette sailed across the study, her slate-blue

gingham dress the only one of the quartet's fashionably long enough. Repeated laundering had turned the garment a peculiar greenish color, much like tarnished copper. She looped her arm through Brooke's.

"Look, dearest." Brette pointed to the tray. "I splurged and made a half-batch of shortbread biscuits. It's been so long since we've indulged, and today is your birthday. To celebrate, I insisted on fresh tea leaves as well."

Brooke would have preferred to ignore the day.

Three and twenty.

On the shelf. Past her prime. Long in the tooth. Spinster. *Old maid.*

She'd relinquished her one chance at love. In order to nurse her ailing father and assume the care of her young sister and three orphaned cousins, she'd refused Humphrey Benbridge's proposal. She couldn't have put her happiness before their welfare and deserted them when they needed her most. Who would've cared for them if she hadn't?

No one.

Mr. Benbridge controlled the purse strings, and

Humphrey had neither offered nor been in a position to take on their care. Devastated, or so he'd claimed, he'd departed to the continent five years ago.

She'd not seen him since.

Nonetheless, his sister, Josephina, remained a friend and occasionally remarked on Humphrey's travels abroad. Burying the pieces of her broken heart beneath hard work and devotion to her family, Brooke had rolled up her sleeves and plunged into her forced role as breadwinner, determined that sacrificing her love not be in vain.

Yes, it grieved her that she wouldn't experience a man's passion or bear children, but to wallow in doldrums was a waste of energy and emotion. Instead, she focused on building a future for her sister and cousins—so they might have what she never would—and allowed her dreams to fade into obscurity.

"Happy birthday." Brette squeezed her hand.

Brooke offered her sister a rueful half-smile. "Ah, I'd hoped you'd forgotten."

"Don't be silly, Brooke. We couldn't forget your special day." Twenty-year-old Blythe—standing with her hands behind her—grinned and pulled a small, neatly-wrapped gift tied with a cheerful yellow ribbon from behind her. Sweet dear. She'd used the trimming from her gown to adorn the package.

"Hmph. Need seedcake an' champagne to celebrate a birthday properly." The contents of the tray rattled and clanked when Duffen scuffed his way to the table between the sofa and chairs. After depositing the tea service, he lifted a letter from the surface. Tea dripped from one stained corner. "This arrived for you yesterday, Miss Brooke. I forgot where I'd put it until just now."

If I can read it with the ink running to London and back.

He shook the letter, oblivious to the tawny droplets spraying every which way.

Mabry raised a bushy gray eyebrow, and the twins hid giggles by concealing their faces in the cat's striped coats.

Brette set about pouring the tea, although her lips twitched suspiciously.

Freddy sat on his haunches and barked, his button

eyes fixed on the paper, evidently mistaking it for a tasty morsel he would've liked to sample. He licked his chops, a testament to his waning eyesight.

"Thank you, Duffen." Brooke took the letter by one soggy corner. Holding it gingerly, she flipped it over. No return address.

"Aren't you going to read it?" Blythe set the gift on the table before settling on the sofa and smoothing her skirt. They didn't get a whole lot of post at Esherton. Truth be known, this was the first letter in months. Blythe's gaze roved to the other girls and the equally eager expressions on their faces. "We're on pins and needles," she quipped, fluttering her hands and winking.

Brooke smiled and cracked the brownish wax seal with her fingernail. Their lives had become rather monotonous, so much so that a simple, *soggy*, correspondence sent the girls into a dither of anticipation.

My Dearest Cousin...

Brooke glanced up. "It's from Sheridan.

Printed in Great Britain
by Amazon